THE BLACK QUEEN STORIES

THE
BLACK QUEEN STORIES

Barry Callaghan

Little, Brown and Company (Canada) Limited
Boston • Toronto • London

First published by
Lester & Orpen Dennys 1982
Vintage U. K. edition 1991

This edition published by Little, Brown Canada 1994.

Canadian Cataloguing in Publication Data

Callaghan, Barry, 1937-
    The black queen stories

ISBN 0-316-12466-4

I. Title.

PS8555.A49B52   1994   C813'.54   C94-931687-3
PR9199.3.C35B52   1994

Printed and bound in Canada by
Best Book Manufacturers Inc.

Little, Brown and Company (Canada) Limited
148 Yorkville Avenue
Toronto, Ontario

For Claire

ACKNOWLEDGEMENTS

The Muscle appeared in *Weekend Magazine* and *Punch.*

Crow Jane's Blues appeared in *Punch, The Punch Book of Short Stories 2,* and *The Ontario Review.*

Spring Water appeared in *Punch.*

The Cohen in Cowan appeared in *Punch* and *Toronto Life.*

Dark Laughter appeared in *Punch.*

The Black Queen appeared in *Punch* and *The Ontario Review.*

All the Lonely People appeared in *Punch* and *Saturday Night.*

A Drawn Blind appeared in *Punch* and *The Punch Book of Short Stories 3.*

And So To Bed appeared in *Exile.*

Silent Music appeared in *Exile.*

On the second day, a sail drew near, nearer, and picked me up at last. It was the devious-cruising Rachel, that in her retracing search after her missing children, only found another orphan.

Herman Melville

The only true madness is loneliness,
the monotonous voice in the skull
that never stops
                    because never heard.

John Montague

Sitting here a thousand miles from nowhere,
People, I'm 'bout to go outa my mind,
Gonna get me a good woman
Even if she's dumb, deaf, crippled or blind.

Buddy Guy

CONTENTS

THE BLACK QUEEN STORIES

Crow Jane's Blues

CROW JANE, WHO WAS A SINGER IN THE LOCAL AFTER-hour clubs, was walking down Spadina Avenue, her hands in her pockets. There were chrome studs on the lapels and cuffs of her jeans jacket. It was nearly midnight but there were five bandy-legged boys playing stickball on the sidewalk in front of the Silver Dollar Show Bar and across the street, in the doorway beside the Crescent Lunch, some immigrant women, probably cleaning-women, were huddled around a homeland newspaper. Their warm laughter touched the loneliness that Crow Jane had felt all week, a loneliness that left her with a listless sense of loss, but she wasn't sure about loss of what, and that was why she was out walking around her old haunts, looking into the show bars from the old days, threading her way through the late night street hustlers who were standing half out in the street between the parked cars, and for a moment she felt good, seeing herself years ago the way she used to slow-walk down the street knowing where everything was, the upstairs bootlegger who kept the beautiful Chinese twin sister hookers who put on a show every midnight, and over on Augusta Street, behind the fruit stalls, there was heavy-jowled Lambchops, the Polish-Jewish giant who hired himself out as muscle to the after-hour clubs. But then, watching a tall white girl in front of a hat shop, the way she primped her hair with pleasure as she caught her reflection in the glass, Crow Jane hunched up and put her head down, suddenly disconsolate. When she looked up the girl was gone.

An empty bus pulled away from the curb and she turned and wandered back up the street, into the Silver Dollar Show Bar where a black girl wearing a silver sequin halter was on the stand. Crow Jane sat in a darkened corner drawing circles on the tabletop in the dampness from ice-cold beer bottles, and as she sat listening, the revolving coloured lights made the singer look like several women at once, all of them afloat in a wash of light, and Crow Jane thought, She's light, lighter than me, and I bet some slicker salesman gave her momma an old black and white TV to see those black breasts and this here's the daughter of that old black and white TV, singing with her head back, eyes shut, opening memories up inside Crow Jane, the night long ago that she wore a dust-rose shirt and had gone up the two flights of stairs on College Street to the small dance hall where two big old women wearing sweatbands and bloated by bad food took tickets at the door. She'd danced with a narrow-hipped, long-legged white girl called EveLynn, and in the lingering light the white girl had said after they'd gone home and Crow Jane had sung for her in a moaning whisper just like this girl singing here in the Show Bar, And yes, she'd said, in the lingering light is where I do like to touch, touch you, ten

4

years ago almost, lying back on the white sheets of the big cannonball bed, her nipples small, the pinky-brown of white women, and yours are plum-coloured she'd said, lying in that bed every night, with her legs spread like a wishbone and, Baby, I said, I got sweetenings, I mean in my time I've sung the song, I been lying up with the shades down just holding on to holding on, but you come high-heel sneaking in your sling-backs into my life and now I got high on sunshine, and the singer on the stand was isolated in a small spotlight, just her face, a black face on a white moon suspended for a moment in the noisy room, But sunshine don't get it all the time 'cause a long time ago it was that I was with you, my little sweetenings, an' we got to always come home to the cabbage, which is why I always to this day every night sing the song how you were my love who brought me the cherry that had no stone, 'cause stones and cabbage is how I most remember my old beat-up hand-me-down days when I be a little girl pedalling my fool self on my tricycle along the long hallway, dead-end, man, I learned early to make the tight turn when you come to the end, so I see this girl so sharp up there in her spotlight of silver sequins looks like me in all the places I already been and turned back from, 'cause you see even my mind got hallways, I mean sometimes I lean back singing a song or lying up with another woman, all the good womens in this world, or poppin' pills, and them pills look like lemon-yellow bowling balls rolling down inside my head, an' sometimes when I get scared, when some sucker comes at me leering with the big hard-on in his eyes, I just sit there talking baby talk we used to talk, me an' EveLynn looking at each other side by side in the mirror, we used to prop the mirror on the bed, that blonde hair of yours on my shoulder an' ever since then I got all the cabbages and none of the kings, an' I been down only the long hallway, pedalling on my tricycle with the bell on the handlebar that don't work, just goes fhzz fhzz like my daddy's old Ronson lighter that got no flint, railroad halls we called 'em, but nobody knows that no more 'cause nobody rides them trains, which is why I like the mouth harp sound, harmonica you called it, white words for black birds, lonesome trains and pain, that was my daddy since back then the onliest work a black man bagged was Pullman porter which my daddy was for a while till insomnia set him down, the clickity-clack inside his head he said, an' I mean he had the light on the whole time, he put pennies on his eyes when he went to sleep an' said I ain't dead, the light jess don't go out, and Crow Jane, listening to the voice on the stand in the small room of the Show Bar, was reminded so much of herself that she decided she wanted to talk to the younger singer, thinking she'd buy the girl a drink, hold her hand a little like she was holding hands with herself, and scribbled a note inviting her to the table. Crow Jane gave it to the waiter. The singer read the note and with a shrug flicked it back behind the piano, And that too is cabbage, Crow Jane said inside her head, boiled cabbage heads, the state of shredded stink, which is bigger than big, all the cabbage-stinking long halls of the world with a raggedy-ann kid on a tricycle going fhzz fhzz at the dead-end dirty window that don't look out on nothing but back alleys, mean mealy living, man, like Daddy drinking whisky which kept his eyeballs on all the time, bulbed outa his headbone before he died, looking on the lookout for what never was, only him always sitting on an afternoon with his hair konked to get it straight, looking at me he'd say, Sweet Thing, when you're black stay back an' if you're brown stick aroun' but if you're white you're right, all that sour self-laughter of his, an' sometimes when I was with that white girl, I think he did tell it true 'cause when she lay there on her side with the lamplight on her hip I knew she was right and I was wrong 'cause I loved her an' black weren't beautiful then, baby, nigger heaven was nowhere, there was just my old daddy sitting on his rusty dusty listening to the *Salt Pork Blues* on the old 78's, his hair straight with lye under the stocking cap and even then, me only being a little girl on the downside of ten, I saw that a grown man sitting with a woman's ugly rolled stocking like a circle of surgical tube on his head was weird, trying to dude himself into the land of seersucker soul, arctic power, whitener was what he was up to an' drove himself stone blind on booze an' left me, little girl sucking wind the day he died, gone down like the light comes up, always the lights come up, ole young girl up there singing so pretty, *I got a baby way 'cross town who's good to me*, and then she stepped down, taking the hand of a lean black man wearing a knitted wool cap, strutting a silver-handled cane and a T-shirt that said SPADE POWER. Crow Jane liked that. I can dig it, I can dig it, and she laughed, wishing that she knew them but it was closing time and people rose and straggled out and Crow Jane suddenly had the feeling that all her past was emptying out of her head, leaving her alone at her table in the corner, staring at the rough ceiling painted black, the water pipes and heating ducts all exposed in the light, And that one time I don't know why me, but they put my picture in the paper, big, full-face, singing at a festival over on the island, an' I felt good an' I said, Daddy, you may be dead and down but there I be, I is, big as lightning on the page for all to see who I am 'cause I am, Crow Jane has sung the song, the fhzz fhzz is finished an' I took that clipping from the paper, an' I said to myself, EveLynn, wherever you are hiding in this here old city with your six kids or whatever, I'm looking you in the eyeball, big, and I am the queen of darktown and I may not be having a ball but I'm still strutting, and I wanted it bigger, so I scissored out that head of myself and took it down to one of them blow-up-yourself picture places an' I say, man, I want this big for framing, hang myself over my head in my bed, two feet by three I said an' he shrugs and when I come back there I am, mounted on cardboard, an' I can't find myself for the looking, my whole face just gone to great big grey and dark dots an' I say, where'd I go, man, I don't see myself at all, an' he says that's what happens when you blow yourself up outa some newspaper, you disappear into dots, man, 'cause if you look close that's all you was in the first place and so the only thing to do was go home, still wanting to take the singer's hand and hold it to her cheek, sweat and perfume on the woman's neck, and to look into the other woman's eyes like she was looking into a mirror, but when Crow Jane went by, walking slowly, it was like there was no silver on the glass, nothing there, and the singer looked right through her, leaving Crow Jane suddenly alone in the doorway, facing the darkness of the street in the cool early morning air. She walked up Spadina. A big milk transport truck rumbled by. She went past a closed restaurant in which a fat-bellied man was all alone swabbing the floors, wearing a stringy undershirt and torn pants, and he waved and when she shrugged with disdain he mouthed a curse at her through the glass. Fog had come in off the lake and she could hear her own footsteps in the empty streets.

A Terrible Discontent

WHEN SHE CAME HOME, THE FIRST THING SHE DID was run her hands through old lacy underclothes in the bureau and put bobby pins into the little porcelain blue bowl she had won at school for elocution, and then she got up on the bed and looked at her legs in the dresser mirror. Men had always said she had good legs, and she smiled, but later standing alone in the street in front of a shop window she saw only her pale face in the glass, and the only life on Luger Street was a preacher down on his hands and knees scratching scripture on the sidewalk with a stub of chalk, and she thought how deeply she had missed men, except now they all seemed like her brother, lanky, underfed, and swimming in a wide, floppy suit coat and trousers, twenty years old and lost in his grey serge postman's suit with the red seam-stripe up the leg.

She was most at ease with herself walking alone on the streets that seemed surprisingly idle and wide, and then down the lanes between houses and back gardens. It had been a dry August and all the yard tomatoes were small, a pink plum size, and the ruts in the lane were filled with white dust, the sun strong on the dead twigs and vines. Someone was burning trash and a crow flew out of the cloud of smoke, settling behind her in the high branches of a silver birch tree. She took a flat stone and threw it at the crow, the stone slashing through the dry leaves, and the bird cawed like raw laughter but she didn't mind the bird's cry: it was people laughing, the chuckling sound they made behind your back that she disliked, and she shook her hair, long and loose, and laughed too, surprised at how loud she laughed, and the bird flew away and she thought there goes the last laugh, those black wings.

She leaned on the old slat gate that hung by one hinge from the garden fence and Simon was there in the shade of the weeping birch tree their father had planted the year Simon was born. Their father had spent weeks under that tree one summer when she was still a high school girl, whittling and carving flutes, and then he had said, There's no point, at least not the point most people think is the point, and soon after some papers arrived in a brown envelope and a little later a lean man wearing flight glasses who shook his hand by the old slat gate, laughing slyly, saying, The beautiful thing is you old soldiers never die no matter how old you get, and the last she had heard, he was somewhere near the equator, probably dead because she got a yellow card postmarked Libreville saying he was *Missing in Action*, which was a funny way of putting it, she thought, for a man lying absolutely still somewhere, and it struck her as she stared at Simon that he had his father's lidded eyes and flat sloping cheekbones, always licking his thin lips, with a smile that might have been shyness but actually was secretive, cunning, which she liked in him, the way he went hunching along the street, shuffling heavy-footed, so big-boned and young, and he surprised her by putting his hand on her shoulder and said that the old woman was in a rage about her not coming back to fix lunch on time and said she was a shirker always trailing trouble like a tin can, and when Collette said she'd hop to it, Yes sir, and made a mocking little motion, waddling like a wind-up doll, he said the old woman had hollered and pounded her cane because Collette was off mooning up the road, which she was, she said, but not mooning, only wondering why she had once thought her star had fallen out of the sky, and she laughed.

The old woman, though she was blind, had always dealt the deck when they played cards at night on the kitchen table, saying since Collette had been a little girl, Grandma's got a right and don't forget that, and when they were children, though Collette didn't know how, the old woman had always snapped the black queen on her, as if she meant it as a mark, and now she was harping and pouting again, insisting that they play as if it were the old days, and when Collette said No, the old woman stomped her feet, tall and stone-blind, eighty-two, and leaning on her blackthorn cane, glaring wide-eyed, her eyes the colour of spit or fish eggs.

Collette hated the old woman's bird that had been with her for years, a guinea cock she kept on a string leash, the nickel-grey feathers shining and the red comb jiggling when it high-stepped in front of the old woman, who threw a fistful of corn, and called out to Collette, You're no good for anyone around here, and clomped up the stairs, her guinea cock alongside her as she eased into the old rocking chair. Collette stood out in the flower garden of foxgloves, poppies, and lilies, looking at the little bits of candy wrapper and an old nylon stocking that were blown up against the wire fence, and she had always wondered how a woman could lose one stocking down a lane, particularly now when women were wearing panty hose, and maybe it was a woman with a wooden leg, she thought and laughed, And wouldn't that be a sight, she said out loud so that the old woman sat upright, erect and listening, but Collette said nothing, enjoying the silence, the sudden expectancy of the old woman, and she looked up and Simon was there with his nose to the back window, watching, and Collette suddenly wasn't quite sure why she had come home to the old iron-haired woman who had always been sour because Collette's mother had died delivering her into the old woman's hands on the kitchen table.

The old woman called out, Get lunch, will you, if you haven't forgotten how, and Collette took a swipe at the poppies with her foot, scattering the petals, and up in the window Simon was smiling and under him on the porch the old woman caressed the neck of her cock. Collette fed the old woman buttered white bread, yellow pea soup, and poached eggs. The sun shone all day. There had been no rain and that night she lay on her bed, hands linked behind her head, a breeze bellying the window curtains and the cool night air left her calm and at ease for the first time in a long while, except she could hear the old woman's rattling snore, the house so quiet that she found herself listening to the creaking beams. The curtains rose and fell like some frail body barely alive and sighing, and she felt a yearning, and not just for a man, because a man could have held her but the way she felt it would have been too hard and unknowing, and how could a man know because she could hardly say herself how she wanted to feel a rush through her loins but no ache, to be touched lightly and lifted like those curtains, bellied up in the air as if they held some living thing and she wondered whether she wanted a child or maybe childhood again, except that she never wanted to be a girl again. There had been so little lace, so little that was childlike in her life, with the bony hand of the old woman always on her, as if by being born she had murdered her mother, and as for her father, until he went away he had acted as if any kindness were a dull brown penny like the old coppers she had flattened when she put them on the railroad tracks, the tracks two blocks away, unused now, the ties over-grown with scrub and weeds, but as a girl she had put her ear to the rails listening to what was far away, and on the day she was told that her father had gone she went along to the old tracks and lay down and cried and listened as if she might hear him somewhere, while the old woman hardly seemed to know he was gone, hard and locked inside herself, the way she had always had hard fingernails, poking into the bedclothes when she was a baby, nails the colour of the underside of a turtle she had once seen over in a pond in the Allan Gardens hothouse which she thought was the loveliest place to be alone in the city, far from the old woman's cold and dry fingers.

Late at night years ago, in some sudden need, the old woman had taken Collette's braided head in her ropy arms and Collette had looked up and seen the loose grey folds of flesh drooping from the old woman's neck, her head high, just like a bird, her old woman's bones sharp and shining in the loose flesh, but except for silent times like that the old woman had carped at Collette and Simon, whom she had always coddled and then ignored with a kind of contempt, just like their father who had been so droop-shouldered, morose, and proud, and always dressed in muddy browns, warming his bare feet before the electric fireplace in the living room during the winter. He had regarded them all with aloof suspicion.

Once, Collette had heard her father tell the old woman, as if he were cheering her up, that there was some unseen meaning in his wife dying in childbirth, that a death cannot mean nothing, and maybe the whole trick, he had said, was in discovering what a death told you to do with your life, and anyway he wanted the old woman to know his wife was his wife for ever and the irony was, Collette thought, that he seemed always preoccupied with sniffing around, a cabinetmaker who had loved the wet feel of stripped wood, the fleshy shine, who had ended up making dozens of little inlaid jewel boxes, stacking them around the house, empty, calling them as a joke his little coffins, and when Collette had said Why, why this sniffing around as if some corner held a clue to where her mother had gone, he had glared at her and said, Someday maybe you'll learn something about losing love, and she had said, I don't intend to lose anything, leaving him alone as he kept busy doing little more than brood, while if anyone in the house asked him a question, any question, he got up and began reading aloud from the newspaper and paraded through the house reading aloud until his anger cooled down, and then he sulked, sorry for them, for himself, burrowing inside himself, and then he went away, an awful thing to do, she thought, so feckless that she wanted to kill someone herself, so she took to dancing and drinking all night, detached from the men she let make love to her, only afraid when she realized that she wanted a baby and didn't care who the father was, and all her disheartened gaiety died, like the breeze in the curtains, the curtains suddenly limp, and she looked up at the ceiling that was so white, so empty, with a spider trekking slowly from the corner. She was going to get up and kill it, but she just lay there, tired and calm, and closed her eyes and went to sleep.

Simon came into her room in the morning and he sat by her feet and laid his left hand on her ankle. He tried to hide that he was watching her breasts. She let the silence hang between them. He took his hand off her ankle and said, What do you think would happen if I were to leave, if I took a room or something somewhere else in the city? There had always been a dulled sensuality about him, some sly cunning to no effect, and she said, I don't know, and Simon leaned forward, elbows on his knees, and said, What I don't understand, and he was licking his thin, almost white lips, is why you haven't gone for good, why you came back and why you're hanging in for a fight with the old woman? Collette said she didn't want to fight with anyone and she felt suddenly saddened and moved by him, sulking around on the edge of his own life, unable to leave home, only half-schooled, which was his father's fault because there had been so much neglect in the family, and so there he was on the end of her bed, slumped forward, a postman, she thought, with a bag full of dead letters, his sallow face staring, and she said to him, I've been alone with aloneness, and I just headed home because home's a point where you can see where you don't want to go again and being somewhere else would be just thirty minutes closer to nothing. She got up and went to the old maple dresser with the oval mirror, and in the rim of the mirror there were yellow curling photographs from just a few years ago, a boy with long hair, Harry something-or-other whose father had owned a pasta store, one smirking face in a row of faces hardly remembered, and she brushed her hair, watching herself and Simon in the old smoky glass and Simon said, You dream about your men I bet. He was crouched forward and his shirt was loose at the throat. She put her hands on his neck, saying, And I bet you've got your naked women in your own mind, and he said, What do you think about? She rubbed his neck, moving her thumbs up his brown burned skin and into his hair, and leaned close so that he could smell her, almost feel her, and knowing that he wanted her hands on him warmed her so much that she was suddenly aware of the dryness in the room, dry wood all through the house, the stairs worn grey and bevelled by so many years of boots up and down except where there were knots standing up like carbuncles, and she could smell the kitchen linoleum, while saying softly to Simon, I sometimes see a man standing straight and his body wet and I run my fingers slowly across his chest, through the hair on his chest. She brushed against Simon's back and then with a little laugh kissed him on the neck and pulled him back against her. That's all, he whispered, so she pulled away knowing she had been unfair, but she stood there shaping her hair with her hands and when he turned, his eyes on her breasts, she hated him for being her brother, and also because he didn't look ashamed at all, and without shame, she thought, we're nothing, and so she went out of the room and opened the porch door and found the old woman asleep, snoring, a rattling whine through the yard, and the string leash had slipped from her hand and the guinea cock was strutting in the dust. She went down into the garden among the lilies and poppies and the headless stems.

She took a pair of hedge clippers and began cutting the stems back and the old woman, with the blackthorn lying between her legs, threw back her head and settled into a steady snore, like a giant insect, Collette thought, and then the old woman came half-awake and groped for the leash. Where's my cock? she cried, and the bird, hearing her, jabbed a leg toward the stairs, and Collette went toward the stairs with the clippers in her hands and the old woman bawled out, Bring me my cock, bring me my cock, but Collette just stood there, uncertain, watching the bird step toward the porch, its head high, and she hooked her foot under its belly and hoisted it into the air and laughed and the cock squawked and flapped and fell head first and the old woman leapt to her feet and screamed, Who's hurting my cock, while the bird whirled with its legs beating the dust and the old woman edged down the stairs, and Simon came banging through the screen door yelling at Collette but she paid no attention, and she and the cock eyed each other, its beak swinging slowly back and forth, the red comb flopping from side to side, its eyes never off her, the old woman yelling behind her as she levelled the clippers and took a step expecting the bird to cut and run but the cock didn't move. There was only the throbbing in the loose flesh of his throat, and when she stood above the bird her hands shook and she could only feel her own blood beating in repulsive time with the bird's stringy neck, and the cock lifted its leg and took one contemptuous step and it was done, a slicing rasp of the hedge clippers. Blood swooshed out of the severed head and the neck and she leapt out of the way, scared, and the cock's body tottered, the blood in bursts, the headless body jagging crazily across the yard, and the old woman, frozen in her blindness, let out a screech as if chanting to the bird in his dance, My cock, my cock, who's hurting my poor cock, and her whole face had collapsed, lips drawn back, baring her yellow teeth, tears down her cheeks, and the cock fell down among the lilies.

Every day afterwards Collette saw the old woman at the upstairs window and sometimes Simon stood beside her. She was in her bedclothes wearing her bedcap and she put her long finger to her lips and then Simon took her from the window. It rained for several days and became so cold that some of the maple leaves turned yellow and red. When Simon came home from work, Collette fed him and then he took a tray to the old woman and sat opposite her while she ate. The old woman did not come downstairs again and Collette told Simon to tell the old woman that she had taken the black queen from the deck, that the little game was over, but the old woman had said nothing, as if, Simon said, she didn't know what Collette was talking about.

Collette began going out alone in the evenings, sometimes taking the old blackthorn cane, which she thought made her appear interesting and elegant because she had read once that a young woman wanting to look mysterious should try to be a little sinister, and she also found a wonderful black cape in mothballs in a bottom drawer, which she thought might have been her mother's. She wrapped herself in the cape in the evenings and once she wore it to a big dance hall, though she didn't bother to go in, but only stood outside listening to the music as if she were waiting for someone and then one evening while she sat in her chair entertaining a boring young man who lived four gardens down the lane, the old woman began rocking above, and he looked up at the noise from the rocking and Collette began to beat out the rhythm of the old woman's rocking with the cane, leaning forward and beating faster on the porch boards as the old woman went faster, trying to lose Collette, and then Collette got ahead of her so that the old woman was trying to keep up with her, and it gave Collette glee, her face glistening, which frightened the young man, but she began to laugh and then all of a sudden the old woman stopped. Tired out I bet, Collette said, and lay back in the chair with the blackthorn between her legs, feeling fine, and in few minutes Simon came down to the porch saying, You should see her, she's as white as a sheet, and Collette said, She should see me, but then she said to her young man, But of course she can't because she's blind, and Simon said, You oughta be ashamed of yourself, and he stomped off and Collette said to her friend, because he was looking bewildered and ill at ease, that he should give her a kiss on the cheek, and he did and then he sat back with his hands folded around his knees and she sat looking out over the garden as the sun went down behind the two-storey houses.

Poodles John

POODLES JOHN OWNED A SMALL CLOTHING STORE. HE was called Poodles because he always carried a little poodle in the crook of his arm. He drove a big white car with old-fashioned fin-tail fenders. He had an easy smile and a little bulge of baby fat under his chin. In the late afternoon, with his car parked by the curb, he liked to stand outside the store wearing a one-button-roll suit — preferably a pearl-grey lightweight flannel — straight-last shoes, a white-on-white shirt, and in the winter, a dark blue Bennie topcoat, narrow at the waist and flared at the skirt. "Today," he always said to his clerks as he strode into the store, "we go for the soft touches."

"You got the touch, Poodles?" his clerks said, laughing.

Poodles John lived with a woman a little older than himself, a handsome woman with auburn hair and full breasts who was in her late thirties. She had a loping walk *and you got racehorse legs* he'd told her, *and good lips, not those razor jobs like some women who'd just as soon cut your heart out*. "And old Luella's got the legs built for speed," she said one morning, smoothing her nylons, "but I'm slowing down. It's not the drop in the tits," she said, "it's under the arms that worries me."

Poodles liked the fullness of her body, remembering his mother before she died, the flushed warmth of her flesh as she sat in front of the mirror listening to an old box radio, keeping what she called, "A little calm before the storm." One soft spring night Poodles yelled, "What goddamned storm?" and she looked at him mournfully. "You only prove you don't know what's out there waiting for us," she said, and Poodles told her he couldn't stand waiting for a bus let alone waiting for what he didn't know was there, and now he had to watch the wary look in Luella's eyes as she sat slumped forward on the side of the bed. He had admired the straight way she walked, her aloofness, and he always tried to walk with his own shoulders thrown back, sure that his ability to keep calm allowed him to handle other men wisely, the way he handled hookers and the clerks in his store. But now she said, "I don't know what I'm going to do."

"About what?"

"About getting old. I'm getting old."

"To me," he said, "you look terrific. We got nothing to worry about, me and you."

"You're such a con artist, Poodles," she said and shook her head. "Like you say. I got the racehorse legs."

"You better believe it, baby."

"I'm going to the glue factory, Poodles."

"This is no goddam glue factory," he said, slamming his hand against the wall. "I ain't no scum-bag and neither are you. I'm telling you to think good about yourself. I think good about myself and I think good about you. If you wanta think bad about yourself, there's nothing no one can do."

He smoothed the lapels of his suit coat. She put her head in her hands. He was worried she was going to cry and he picked up the poodle and went out, driving slowly downtown, and he took two deep calming breaths as he strode into the store carrying the dog. His clerks called out, "You got the touch today, Poodles?" He put the dog in its hamper behind the counter. "I always got the touch," he said, and the two clerks laughed. "Magic man, that's me," and he was pleased, going upstairs to the room over the store, but as he stepped into the grey light of the bare room and saw the unpainted walls, the day-bed and the card table, the phone and the slat blinds, all his good feeling drained away *and it's all her fucking fault the bitch.*

Poodles closed the blinds. He ran a poker game in the afternoon in the upper room. He was a good dealer, sternfaced and his fingers always fast, and he broke open a new Bicycle deck and a carton of cigarettes. A long time ago an old dealer named Herschel, who never drank liquor but still died of cirrhosis of the liver, told him to give players a little something free. "It's a touch," he told him, "and they think they're among friends, and there's no one you can fade faster than a guy who thinks he's among friends." Poodles set out tinfoil pouches of potato chips along with the cigarettes. Emptying the ash trays, he sat down, worried about Luella who'd become so erratic, breaking into tears that left him speechless, and he'd had enough of keeping his mouth shut all his life *what with all the shit and trouble it took to get a fistful of anything* and he remembered bitterly when only a few players had come in the door and he'd had to scuffle and scramble, running the game for a big Greek who had fronted all the money, always trying to skim something for himself while trying to run the game and take a little betting action on the phone at the same time. The players had complained about the phone ringing and he had sweated a lot. He'd stuck his betting slips, little roll-your-own cigarette papers, to his sweating arm while laying cards around and nobody liked that, *and that was the ass end of it all,* Poodles said, remembering how the Greek had come by and taken a lady's lipstick mirror from his vest pocket and hunched forward on the day-bed clipping his razor moustache with small scissors, saying, "You're in the phone book, Poodles. You're Poodles Enterprises, but you're not turning shit. You take in loose change that don't pay the rent. You think, eh? You think what to do Poodles, but until then, no more front money. You're on your own with your dinky dog. Do me a favour, eh? Get rid of the dog. It's humiliating, a big man with such a little dog. It's unnatural."

But Poodles had opened up on his own, working three hookers in the Pearlmutter Hotel. He liked his girls, and one of them, Carrie, a girl with corn-yellow hair and small breasts, had real talent. Men asked for her and he appreciated her talent. He wanted his girls to do well, and one day when he was sitting with Carrie in her hotel room, her Kleenex box and washcloth on the floor beside the bed, he told her she was terrific and that she had real talent, and it was too bad, he said, that she wasn't better looking so that she could have made a big buck, and she only smiled and said, "Well, what're you going to do? You

24

do the best you can." Poodles had been touched and at the end of the week he gave her an extra fifty dollars because he now had six girls working for him and he laughed and said, "Never give a sucker an even break," *and suddenly I'm right where I want without really trying which is I got a string of girls and my own ass ain't on the line in my own premises so maybe I should say to myself that me and Lou should take a holiday* while at home Luella hung around looking glum and sometimes when he came up the walk he saw her staring out the window *like one of those women in ghost movies always staring out the upstairs window* and one night he came upstairs and stood quietly beside her, looking down into the street through the thick leaves of a crimson maple. There was a light breeze. "Beautiful," he said. Someone had cut the grass and he could smell the sweetness. "Just take a whiff of that," he said, touching the small of her back. Then the man who owned the house came down the street holding hands with a willowy black girl and Poodles said disdainfully, "Jesus, even I draw the line at coons. No self-respect, man." Luella shrugged, indifferent to the little distinctions he drew between himself and other men. "Sometimes," he said, "you treat me like I'm any low-class hustler," and because his business was bigger he knew he wasn't ordinary and so he worried more about her when she refused to laugh at his deprecating jokes and she made him feel that he had no right to believe he was a shrewd respectable businessman. "I worry about you all the time, baby," he said, but she only said she was going out for a walk.

At the end of the week he took her to Puerto Rico. It was the off-season and too humid and hot, but she'd been so morose around the apartment, staying out later and later at night, that he had decided to get out of town. But in the morning he woke up and found her staring into the mirror as if they were still at home.

"Jesus, Lou. Six thousand miles and the sun's out and you're sitting inside in the dark."

But she was watching him in the mirror and he was taken aback by the mournful, almost pitying look in her eyes. He brushed his hair back with the flat of his palms. "What are you doing, eh?" he asked as calmly as he could.

"I was thinking about my father."

"And what?"

"He was a good man."

"So he was a good man. That got him a cup of coffee."

"Aw, Poodles, don't you ever think about your dad? Don't you ever think about anyone?"

"I think, baby," he said, alarmed because she sounded as if she felt sorry for him. "All the time I think about you, I got you on my mind like a brick, and the question ain't what I'm thinking but how come you're thinking what you're thinking, which I don't know about although I'm the guy you live with, but all of a sudden I'm the guy you don't talk to."

"That's funny," she said. "My father didn't talk to me either. Hardly ever."

"So maybe he had nothing to say."

She threw her shoulders back and smiled, but he felt a little chill, the short hairs bristling on his neck, and she stroked her throat and said, "All my childhood my father gave me dolls, Punch and Judy dolls and puppet dolls on strings, and he'd dance the dolls in the air inside a box and they had big glass eyes, staring eyes like insane flowers that followed me all around my bedroom, and years later you know, some nights when we used to go dancing with the spotlights in the mirror behind us, the spotlights looked like big flower eyes and sometimes I felt so high like I'd done some dope and felt filled with petals spinning there in the eyes of all the faces watching me."

The wistful longing in her voice made him reach out, surprised at his open extended hand, the puffy flesh, surprised at his sudden arousal, and he said, "I want you, Lou."

"Yeah but do you want my mother?"

"Who's talking about your mother?" he said sourly, feeling rebuffed.

"That's the point. My father never talked about my mother. She went off when I was a kid and he refused to ever talk about her. Said such talk would only hurt us."

"So?"

"So, the more and more I look in the mirror the more it's like I'm finding my mother."

"Jesus H. Christ," he said. He got out of bed, wanting to shake her by the shoulders, yet what he really wanted was to lie back and let her make love to him, so he stood behind her, seeing himself naked in the mirror, pudgy and white and vulnerable, but she looked up at him and said, "It's like someone's moving in on me, another face, and I'm sure it's her face. I mean I'm nearly forty and when I'm forty I'll look in the mirror and know who my mother was."

That afternoon she sat alone and out of the sun. She

was silent and wore big black sunglasses. He couldn't tell what she was looking at. He was wounded and said, "You know what you look like? One of them women in movies whose husband's just been killed, sitting in church, you know, funeral wop, eh!" He laughed but she only touched her throat and he stared at the empty swimming pool. It was an acid green, a polished shining surface that hurt his eyes, and he said, "Goddamn, this is crazy. There's no one swimming." He leapt in awkwardly and when he bobbed back to the surface, he called out, "You do what you do, baby, but don't do it to me. Don't do what you're doing to yourself to me."

That evening in the casino, when he lost money at the crap tables, he said nothing but blamed her. She had killed his good feeling, his glow *like I knew when I walked in the door the glow was gone and the man in the monkey-suit smiled at me like I had loser written all over my kisser* and he'd thrown the dice with no confidence. He'd had no luck and he lay awake in bed beside her, angry as the whirring air conditioner drowned out the sound of the sea, and then she blurted out, "I always wanted to try hang gliding, that's what I wanted to do, just like you see in the movies, that's the way I wanted it. It must be perfect, drifting on the air currents like that, all alone up above everything, totally silent in the sun, just hanging there, the whole world clear. I read somewhere that that's what it's like if you die, and then you don't die but come back."

Poodles lay in the dark with his hands folded on his chest. "Yeah, and me," he said, "I wanted to be a winner, in a big way I wanted to be a winner and instead I take a beating for two thousand and end up in bed with an out of work hang glider."

"You know what Poodles?" she said, leaning over him so that her long hair brushed his bare chest, "You and the dog are a real team, you know that? You're going to end up with a dog in a basket. How about that?"

"So what?" he cried, leaping away from the frightening touch of hair moving across his body. "Who gets laid around here anyway?"

He turned off the air conditioner and went out alone to the balcony, saying, "So sweat! Take a little heat. You can stand to shed some weight."

"You bastard," she cried, "you'll be sorry." He was sorry, yet he said nothing more because he'd already said too much, and he sat in the plastic deck chair listening to the roll of the sea and the next day they went home.

As weeks went by, he spent more time in the store needling his clerks and running his game and his girls and hustling cheap suits off the rack. He left ties, shirts, cuff links and socks to the clerks. "That's what clerks are for," he said. "The extras, and always they should remember they're also the extras." Cradling the little dog, he referred to himself as an outfitter. "What you call yourself is what you are, at least as far as I'm concerned," he said to the clerks. He didn't let his clerks get close to him, but he was avuncular with his hookers, thinking he had a special touch with women and that he knew how to handle them. He called the girls, who were lean and young, his ladies of the evening, "And ladies," he said sternly, "there's always a fat man trying to get into a thin woman and we want some fat for ourselves."

He met the girls once a week in the Mercury Club. It was a bar with a small dance floor and a juke box owned by an ex-boxer who was now a referee who wrote angry letters to the newspapers supporting capital punishment. It was a bar popular among men in their late thirties and early forties and he gathered the girls in the early evening when the bar was almost empty. Moxie Mensler the boxer would sit down for a moment, take his edge money in a little brown envelope, and then a waiter brought raw hamburger on a saucer. Poodles fed meat pinched between his forefinger and thumb to the dog as the girls came in and sat down. They smiled at the dog and one, who liked to wear a man's tie and suit coat during the day, surprised them because she had knitted little wool pouches for the dog's paws, like little mittens for the winter, and now the girls all brought ribbons or little strings of bells. Poodles liked the tone of these early evenings and he felt like a solid businessman *because I'm my own fucking man with collateral and collateral makes the man in other men's eyes* which is why the other day the bank manager in the branch he had banked in for a decade had suddenly come through the gate and taken his hand, wishing him well. At first, Poodles had been afraid that something was wrong, but then he was pleased that he had kept his calm after the man's hand came out to him like a confirmation, a blessing, because, he had told Luella later, a bank manager is the one man who really knows how things add up. Poodles, standing there in the hush of the small bank branch, had decided to open up a new store.

But Luella had little to say. He thought she was in a sleepwalk, and then she would suddenly tell him strange stories about her father and how he had always calculated his life according to magic numbers: 5 . . . 8 . . . 17 . . . 28 . . . . "Who told him they were magic?" she said sternly, "And why would he believe it when the only magic he ever made was making my mother disappear out of his life?" Poodles thought for a moment and then said, "Every sucker's got a system. I got smarts." She stared at him sullenly and then smiled, as if she had seen him in a new light. "That's right," she said, "you're too smart to get sucked in by anybody's magic, Poodles," and she went out, as she did nearly every afternoon, to a private ballroom-dancing class where she said she was spun around elegantly by a young, slightly effeminate man who sometimes kissed her hard on the neck as he folded her back in his arms *and she's got the nerve to tell me the only time she's treated elegant is by some lousy fag hustling in a dancing school it's so corny it's disgusting.* "And boys," he said to the clerks one day, "let me give you a little piece of Poodles' advice. The only way to handle women is leave 'em alone. Let 'em make up their own minds and then you don't get blamed for nothing, 'cause that's what most people get off on, is blame, to make you feel smaller than they feel small."

The clerks shuffled uncertainly in front of Poodles who was slumped in his chrome chair, lost in his own thoughts until a man came in the front door wearing glasses and worn shoes. Poodles smiled, flattening his wide tie on his stomach. Suddenly at ease with himself, he took the man warmly by the elbow to the rack of charcoal-grey suits, and then moved him into the corner mirrors and tapped him on the bottom and tucked him under the armpits. "Touch, touch till they're on their toes," he had told his clerks, "it's the privates, they're all worried about their privacy, but you got 'em up against the wall until you let 'em down real slow into $99.50, letting on like you believe in good grooming, and then $90 flat, wear it home, put what you got on in a box."

A little flushed and relieved to step away from the mirror and Poodles' soft touch, the man put on the suit and said "Yes, yes, it's wonderful," and went out with his old clothes under his arm in a box, pausing to look at a more expensive sharkskin suit on one of the window dummies, and then he walked away in the afternoon light. Poodles sat back in his chrome chair, satisfied, sure that he knew how to size up a man and he said, smiling, "You watch, the first fucking rain and that suit'll go up like a window blind."

The clerks laughed appreciatively and Poodles sat with his hands crossed on his breast, basking in their admiring laughter. Then he reached down and picked up the little dog and stroked its small nose with his forefinger. "See," he said, "how good old poppa Poodles is when he's going good." In the late afternoon he drove home slowly, satisfied that he was right to think well about himself. The dog was in a basket-woven hamper in the front seat. It was a misty humid evening and the sun was a brilliant red. He shielded his eyes and drove a little faster.

Luella had laid out cold cuts covered with Saran-wrap on the table in the alcove dining room. She was buttoning a black chiffon blouse and looked slim and tailored in a black skirt and black alligator pumps.

"So," he said, "who's the funeral for?" She shrugged and said, "I'm going out."

"Out, out," and he put down the dog, "what's out? Always these days you're on your way out, and every day you're got up more and more like a Turkish delight. What the hell's going on?"

"I'm getting my act together."

"You got an act? So where's your act?"

"Very funny."

"Who said funny? You call what you been doing an act. A bad actor okay, but take it on the road and you can forget it."

"I'm going out."

Outraged and afraid that if he threw her out to save his own pride she would never come back, he touched her shoulder, trying to surprise her with concern, but instead he scowled and said, "Calm down."

"I'm calm," she said.

"Yeah, but calm down."

"What is this? How calm can I get?"

"What do you want to do to us?" he asked. "What do you want to do to yourself?"

"What you don't do," she said.

"So what's to do?"

"I want to feel fresh, all right."

"Fresh. Fresh is for fruits, which is what you're maybe hanging around with too much."

"Inside, Poodles. I want to feel fresh inside."

"So feel, who's stopping you?"

"Nobody, Poodles. Nobody's going to stop me, that's the point. So lemme by, okay."

"To where?"

"Out."

"Ten years we live together and now it's out like I don't get no rights."

"I'm going to Gimlet's."

"Gimlet's! What are you, crazy?"

"Sure I'm crazy. Old crazy legs is stepping out."

"A goddamn dog'd go in that joint with his nose in the air."

She slammed the door and he cried, "You cheat on me and I'll break your legs. I'll take a baseball bat to your legs." He could hear her step fading on the stairs. "Stick crape on your nose," he yelled again, picking up a piece of salami. "Your brains are dead."

Poodles settled into his easy chair feeling sour. The phone rang and he took a bet on a baseball game in Cleveland. Then he sat alone in the silence, suddenly aware of the hum of the air conditioner, and he was reminded of Puerto Rico, and he wished that it had all gone differently, and maybe he should have talked to her about his mother, too. Maybe that would have cheered her up. He ate very little and poured himself a drink. He cradled the dog and stroked the back of its head. "It's like she don't expect me to be angry," he said aloud to the dog. "What the fuck's that all about?" The dog licked the palm of his open hand. He poured himself another drink and went out on the porch and sat on the small love seat they'd bought for summer nights. The sun was going down behind the garage roofs.

He tried to imagine Luella sitting at the cramped tables in Gimlet's, slapping the flat of his hand on the armrest of the love seat because the night he'd gone there he'd stared at a long-legged girl who had a flat belly and narrow hips and small hard breasts, and he had been filled with a lust that left him surprised, and her small behind with the little bush of black hair when she bent over had seemed so vulnerable that he'd said to himself, "Jesus, I'd kiss that," and then, afraid that he'd spoken out loud, he had got up and hurried home, *but all those randy pinstripers just hang around,* he thought, *and when the girls go backstage they'll fall all over any real woman,* especially Luella with her aloof air, the way she held her head as if nothing in the world could startle her, and he leaned forward suddenly seeing her as a seductive woman who knew exactly what she wanted and how she was going to get it. "Goddamn," he said, and then he wondered if she really had gone to Gimlet's. Maybe she had gone to the Twenty-Two, which was possible, because she had mentioned models and something about a young film producer and he'd only half-listened to her, thinking she was talking about dancing classes, but the Twenty-Two was the place these days for film hacks and *my God for all I know she's into flicks* and he realized that he had no idea where she was or what she was doing and he felt betrayed, and then helpless. "You got to always sleep with one eye open," he said bitterly. He poured another drink, closed his eyes, and said quietly, "We had the world by the short hairs."

He saw a woman sitting alone on a back porch dressed in a white halter and white slacks. She seemed to be watching him, too, and he suddenly waved the bottle of rye and she waved back. He pointed, suggesting he should come over, and she waved again. He got up, a little excited, saying to himself, "Goddamn, I'm gonna steal me some pussy." He picked up the dog and went down the wooden back stairs into the darkening cinder alley between the garages and then he was out in the narrow laneway, sure that if he counted four or five garage doors to the left he would find the right alley into the woman's yard, but each opening was so shadowed he couldn't be sure, and then he was in almost total darkness as he half-trotted from alley to alley, staring up at empty porches.

He took a drink from the bottle and decided to go home. The dog was whimpering. He hunched over and began to walk very fast. Someone yelled, "Hold it right there." There was a blinding light in his eyes and then the light was lowered and he saw two cops standing back in the shadows of an open garage door and one said, "A little early for peeping, eh fat fella?"

"What the hell you talking about?"

"We're talking about you."

"The hell you are, I'm no damned peeper."

"Sure, sure," the cops said. "You're just sneaking around behind houses with a bottle of cheap whisky because you and your dog got nothing better to do."

"It's goddamn expensive whisky," he said, full of resentment, but for some reason he found himself remembering his mother sitting beside her radio listening every Sunday to a man named Mournful Smith who whistled songs while playing the piano. He could see the polished black toecaps of the cops' boots and suddenly wary, backing away from the light, he said, "I ain't up to nothing."

"Give us the whisky," one of the cops said. Poodles handed him the bottle and the dog leapt out of his arms, yapping at the heels of the cops, and one of the cops whirled Poodles around and up against a wall, kicking his legs apart.

"For Christsake, get your hands off me," he cried.

"We got a touchy peeper." The cop began to handle his hips, getting up close to him. "And call off your dog," the cop said and laughed.

"Look, I got a business. I live just down the lane."

"Yeah, and what do you do?"

"I'm an outfitter."

"A what?"

"An outfitter."

"What's that, a plumber?"

"I make suits."

"You know what I can't understand," the other cop said. "How come you guys fool around back alleys when there's all that naked quiff in the bars downtown?"

"I was looking for someone," he said. "There was someone waiting for me out there." He scooped up the dog. The cop opened his wallet and took out a card. "Ignatius John Tacoma. What do you do, Tacoma?"

"I own a clothing store. Where else do you think I'd get a good-looking suit like this."

"Stand straight and turn around," one cop said.

"Okay, so I'm straight."

"Maybe you're queer?" the cop said.

"You don't got no call to insult me," Poodles said. "All I want's to be left alone. I got my privacy."

"How come," the cop said, "if there's nothing wrong you're sweating so much?"

"Who's sweating?" Poodles said. "I'm very calm."

"Yeah, how calm?"

"How calm can I get?" he said, squinting into the flashlight. "I got nothing to worry about."

"We'll see," the cop said.

Poodles put up his hand, shielding his face. "What's to see?" he said, but now that the glaring light was out of his eyes, he saw that both cops were very young, almost baby-faced, and he was furious that he'd let himself be handled so easily. "Just like a fucking window blind," he said.

"What?" one cop said.

"None of your damn business," he cried. "If I wanta spend my whole goddamn life down a back alley it's none of your business."

He was so angry with himself that there were tears in his eyes. "Lou'd just love to look at this," he said, and he turned to see if her face wasn't there in the window.

"Who is Lou?"

"Wouldn't you like to know," Poodles said contemptuously.

"Go on home," one of the cops said. "Get your act together," and both cops stepped back into the dark.

"You call this an act," he yelled. "This is no goddamn act," and he shook his fist at the shadows. The cops didn't answer.

"You're crazy," Poodles cried, cradling the dog. The dog was licking his hand. "You got your dumb flashlights but you got nothing on me." One of the dog's little woolen mittens was missing. He didn't know how he could explain to the girls how he'd lost the mitten. "You don't see nothing," he cried, looking again for her face in the window. "You don't see nothing, 'cause I got collateral, man. I got collateral."

Anybody Home?

LEONARD CHOLET WAS A LEAN OLD DOCTOR IN HIS late seventies who had dyed black hair and a domed forehead. He wore loose, double-breasted suits with padded shoulders. He unbuttoned my shirt, tapping my chest, listening to my heart. "To you," he said, "a pounding heart is a problem. To me, a long time ago a heart murmur was more than I could hope for." Unopened envelopes cluttered his desk. I could feel his breath on my cheek. He tapped again. "Anybody home?" and the old man laughed, saying, "Don't listen to me. I talk because there's nothing else to do at my age. You should listen to your own heart, eh? How's that for a little truth, except most people nowadays try to think with their head instead of their heart." He had a perfectly pressed three-point white handkerchief in his breast pocket. The old floor creaked as he walked back and forth. I closed my eyes. For a moment there was silence. I lifted my hands. "What you got there?" he said. I opened my eyes and looked around. "Where?" I said. He laughed. "Between your hands, you look like you're holding something." I shook my head. "Memories, maybe?" he said, "I got memories. Memories are made of what you're looking at, me, what I hold on to." He took a flat wooden stick and his stainless steel pencil-light and said, "Open your mouth. I got to look inside. You're tense, you know that. For a guy that looks so calm you're very tense." I closed my eyes again, listening to his creaking floors, creaking footsteps, my own footsteps last night as I crossed her parquet floors, *the walls white and the floors loose from dampness and there was only a tubular table holding the TV in the room,* "And say ah," the old doctor said, *dampness from it being in the basement,* "Ah," *and the white plastic padded headboard, foam-filled pillows, and she sighed, lay back and sighed so luxuriously, slate eyes, breasts lolling to the side, hips narrow, and small delicate feet, discreet little cries like being half-ashamed,* "Ah," *and then blowing smoke, saying that at home around the house she liked to wear a Blue Jays ball cap when she hunkered up late at night doing her nails, hummed out of her skull, she said, by evangelical television shows, and she always slept till about ten, sleeping healthy, she said, "see, look, no stress marks, that's the selfsame pure skin I was a born baby with."*

"But the only link," Cholet said, "with those years after the war, you hear what I'm saying, is my son, who's now like a big boot. With a hole in it. There's nothing wrong with your throat, but with him and his heart, there's something wrong. See, he likes to wear those yellow construction-worker boots with little steel clips on the toes but me, I keep to my slippers with the sponge soles and my room with the lamplight like a little escape hole in the darkness, but for him, the way I look at it, it was a mistake my making a marriage, a man like me." He put the stethoscope, which reminded me of the black gumdrops I loved as a boy, into a case and snapped it closed, saying, "A man like me should never have married, but anyway she pretty soon went away leaving my son to do something big, to live." The alarm clock went off, a tone-less bleeping, and Cholet hit the clock with the flat of his hand, big-boned through the shoulders, and he turned away, making pencil notes in his little pocket book. "You got a heart like a horse, so what's to worry for you?" I looked up at an old pewter lamp hanging from the centre of the ceiling, six sockets empty. Cholet, standing with one hand in his suit coat pocket, lean and severe in the shadow-light, put his notebook away, saying, "I give you more powerful pills, don't worry, you want to calm down, you'll calm down." He snapped a wooden match on his thumbnail and lit a Gitanes, inhaling deeply. "So now this son of mine," he said, handing me my shirt. "He owns pigeons, some homing pigeons he tells me, cages up on top of the roof, and he says no matter what he does to them, doesn't feed them, twists a wing, it doesn't matter, they always come home to him, and others he's got are called carriers. To me, it sounds like a disease. He sends messages to I don't know who, maybe no one *settling down in her underpants with little wing bows, sparrow wings if they could fly, bare-breasted at her table, polish-remover bottle open, and spread fingers on the table, long nails, rubbing them clean, the cap pulled down over her eyes:*

"Sometimes I put in a case of beer and a guy comes by, you don't mind me telling you, eh, I mean we know what's the score, a little girl's got to be with a man every now and then but always they got that question, you know, moon-faced they look at you asking, was it good, was I the best? but never

saying love, never a little love word, "Ah," and the last guy standing in the doorway on the way out, that's what he wanted to know before he can go, so I says, at least you got your dry-goods store Henry and at least you're a good bowler and his eyeballs popped like I poleaxed him. Anyway, what I worry about is my nails. If you ever been a typist, you know those big rooms all carpeted for quiet and a hundred girls plugged into headsets, the only thing breaking the rhythm is someone breaks a nail, but what you got to face is it's always guys who are already losers who got to ask that question, you know, Was I good? which they've been asking since they got off the tit and onto apron strings, just losers, which we all are anyway, you play the game and you throw boxcars, you crap out, and maybe it's wrong, but it comes up boxcars and standing by the window, Cholet, his coat rumpled from sitting all morning in his chair, hooked his forefinger into the ring on the dark green window blind and with a little tug he ran the blind up, letting in the late afternoon light. He blinked and shied away from the light while I buttoned my shirt, standing in the shadows. "You've got a good heart, so look after it," he said. "I will walk out with you."

Going down the stairs, a light scarf knotted at his throat because there was a chill in the air, he stopped on the bottom stair and took hold of my elbow, almost affectionately, and suddenly I felt a tenderness, and he shook his head, saying, "The whole thing was a mistake, that's the truth, the big thing is maybe life itself is a mistake, God made a mistake, he didn't intend any of this, but somehow it works out in its own way, like my little table and desk, nice pine pieces, twenty years ago I bought old chairs and things like that, secondhand, and one day a man who never paid a bill, just did odd jobs to look after his debts, he said, While you're away Monsieur Cholet, I'll fix the furniture and when you come back you won't know where you live." There were breadcrusts thrown on the lawns and grey pigeons pecked at the crusts. Laundry had been hung on a front porch and two black women wearing bandanas were gathering fruit and tomatoes that had fallen out of a torn shopping bag. Cholet walked the inside line of the sidewalk, holding close to the walls. "I was going away, you see," he said, "for two weeks to fish, because one thing I like about this country is the dark water, back in a cove where it's calm like you can see the dust floating and this man, he said while I was away he'd clean off the thick old paint so I'd see how beautiful the wood was, and for two weeks I sat in my boat in the rain and came back to the tables and chairs all waxed a honey-color, a room full of junk wood looking like a treasure, and he was right, I didn't know where I was, and he said to me, beaming, happy, Monsieur Cholet, he said, now these are just like you had roots"

her spread fingers, leaning on her elbows, working the little brush, cotton ball buffing her nails, very calm and half-naked, wearing the baseball cap, and high-heeled shoes lined up along the baseboard of the wall that had one window at lawn-level to the street, some shoes expensive and some fluorescent satin and rhinestone clusters on the toes. "I got the inside line on losers," she said. "Every day I listen to twenty losers at the hairdresser's, ladies under the hair dryers who like to gamble, you know, place a bet with the manicurist who's a tout for some bookie because it's private, you know, gambling is private like playing with yourself, get a tense little high with every bet, take a risk. I once knew a girl who could just cross her legs and squeeze hard and get a rush, the flush of the rush. You come down, go up, like in escalator land. I walked along with Old Cholet because I had nothing to do. I had no one at home. *It beats boredom. I mean what's more boring than crossing your legs all day," she said, blowing her nails under the lamplight, hands almost a man's but long, tapered and beautiful like clean bones in the light, and holding them out, palms up, spread fingers, "See, I'm clean, got nothing to hide," and she laughed and clapped her hands, a whack hollow in the white room. "You know those shoes," she said, standing up, "I don't wear them nowhere, not even when I'm dancing 'cause I just like trying them on. I put on some nylons, you know, expensive, and a garter belt and slip them on like I was a man looking down at myself trying on ladies' shoes, except I'm the lady so I get a double rush, action both ways, which is the gambler's dream, a win-win situation, so I can't lose"*

Though old Cholet had been in his rented rooms for years, no one seemed to know him. He passed Ram's Curry Shop and Sam Mi's Trading Company, the walls hung with a hundred wigs and hairpieces. "Anyway," he said, holding up his hand like a cop as he walked out into the street, "before the war I was a doctor in a part of Paris where there were clothing and sewing shops, poor and mostly Jewish, but I wasn't Jewish, and I had a second-floor office up off a lovely wrought-iron stairwell painted white, like iron lace, and marble stairs and an office all frosted glass panels with pansies etched into the glass, a horsehair couch, and the first naked woman I saw, ever, was in that frost light, absolutely still she stood and I walked around and around her stunned by this blackness between her legs, hair like the root of darkness, and then soldiers came a few years later and herded all the Jews and me too, they came right into my home and took me off to the trains." He held me by the elbow again. "You know, you're a good listener," he said. "But the trouble with a good listener is you don't know for sure whether he's listening." He laughed and I said, "What can I say?" as he stepped into the grey light of the Parthenon Room and said, "Anyway, I was no Jew, I went into a rage in circles, dancing, how could they do such a mistake, and terrified I told them to take down my pants, they'd see, and when they didn't I did, I held my cock, my own self out to them like an offering, my proof," and he sat down with his back to the wall, facing the stage in the big empty restaurant. There were plastic olive-coloured leaves and grapes hanging from crossbeams over the bar. The jukebox was playing and two north-country Indians were sitting alone in a corner, aimlessly rolling red dice along their tablecloth, calling out the numbers. "You see, I look back," he said, "it's like one day watching, because nothing could be hidden in the camps, a young boy and girl making love, and they had the skin and bones of old, old people, looking like they would have looked if they'd lived a long life, and they made love furiously, whispering over and over love words and making love like lunatics, nearly killing themselves because they had no more life coming and some of us watched and we knew what they were doing, killing themselves off quicker, which in a way we envied because we kept our hearts hidden, but otherwise I don't remember much except for the sound of the boxcar wheels clicking on the rails, that doesn't go away, and baby shoes, piles and piles of little shoes, and I'd seen men slide off what we called the flute, the board with the bum holes over the cess pit, fall off into the shit and drown, a terrible thing, a man swallowing shit, and later after I was out and on my feet, I'd lost an eye but I felt good because again I could smell tobacco on myself, and I bought a suit, a good suit, heavy tweed, brown but with a green thread all through so it looked almost dark green, and I had this one eye with an eye-patch and sometimes I found myself standing staring at myself in shop windows like the windows were mirrors and before I got myself out of Paris I thought I'd get a glass eye. I was blue-eyed but I got a green eye to match my good Sunday suit which seemed right in a wrong kind of way, like a joke on a joke, like for a while I ate only kosher food, awful tasting stuff, a non-Jew more Jewish than the Jews, but now I eat anything, junk food, it doesn't seem to matter"

as she walked over to the window wall and stepped into purple suede pumps, laughing and parading, then planting herself and angling her left foot like she was on stage, chin up, mockery-full of herself and full of nakedness and silence in the room, the feel of eyes, my smile, all the approval needed, and she said her father'd had his own dream about her too, "'cause he was in construction, and he loved being the boss 'cause he said life is for steadfast guys, that's the way he talked, and he wanted nothing to do with windsucker guys, guys who had small dreams and held on to them. He made model airplanes, you know, paper and balsa wood, and he went into all these big summertime competitions on the island, trying to win and betting he would win. He was a big bettor on himself, money talks and bullshit walks, is what he said. So one day another flier says to me, can he have a date and before I can say yes or no my old man says his daughter don't go out with no windsucker guys and laughs himself blue saying

Walk, Walk, which was the nicest thing my father ever said about me," and down she sat with her legs stretched, still wearing the baseball cap, staring and then said, *"It's all a gamble, look at me, where I ended up, a hairdresser, and I bet everyday,"* she said, *"you'd be surprised how many women are throwing their bread away every day just to get a little action in their lives. You'd be surprised what's humming under the hair driers, but I lose like everyone else except one day I parlayed a real payoff into some big bucks and I decide the hell with it, time to come up in the world, move out of this here basement and across the street, top floor in the highrise, so I take a place after talking to the Super and I got no furniture, which you can see, so he says he'll help carry what's around, and I know he's hoping for a little action with me himself so he's got the mattress, a single, you know, and I got the box-spring, which weighs nothing, and he get it across the street and I'm coming and then right in the middle of the road carrying a goddam box spring a car hits me* "But what happens," Cholet said, "even when there's nothing, what we called nothing, and this is remarkable enough in itself to live for, is even in the camp we played cards, we played with little dirt-marked cards, all the one-eyed kings and jacks passed hand to hand, a little luck, good or bad, so strange, the way we become what we have shared," and he smiled, crossing his skinny legs.

"What I mean is, now there are four of us. We're not friends necessarily, but we found each other here in this city which we'd never heard of before, men lucky to be alive anywhere, nobodies from nowhere, three Jews and me, and what am I? Nothing, and it's our home but not our home, so there we are playing cards every Friday night with a man who's our pharmacist in a highrise, a young Chinese, very nice with all white rooms with white rugs, a round table. He plays poker almost every night, this Chinese, it seems gambling's in their blood, and stacked on the floor against the wall a foot deep on one side of the table are *Playboys* and *Penthouses* from ten years back and the same thing on the other wall, except it's *Popular Mechanics*, and if your cards are no good, you sit and take your choice thumbing through these books *She laughed hard, circling the table, high heels clacking on the loose parquet floor, pulling her cap over her eyes, naked arms open, "I ask you, someone who gets hit by a car carrying a box-spring is in big trouble, right, that's boxcars when you get hit while hustling a bed in the middle of the road, I mean that's a signal, man, so I moved right back down here into the basement, I mean this is where I live, the most roots I got I guess, and I never gambled since because when you get a sign you got to go with it. No highrise for me. So I'm easy, very okay, I don't break my nails, I don't break my heart, I'm a good dancer and I got some nice shoes, right"* A young girl strode out of the kitchen, a jacket of beads and tassels draped over her bare shoulders. Cholet ordered saganaki and a salad of black olives and onions in oil. "Black olives with good spices, you know how hard they are to find?" he said. "No," I said, and he said, "Say Ah," and laughed. I laughed, too, and opened my mouth. He shook his head and smiled. "I like you. A little tense but all right. You would've been okay where I was. And here you're okay, too. So what's to worry. You got a heart like a horse."

The small stage was spotlit for the girl. Her cigarette burned to the filter-tip in an ash tray while she danced. She clomped around in a circle, sometimes cupping her breasts, chewing gum. The Indians paid no attention, laughing, rolling the dice, calling numbers. "This doesn't go on long," Cholet said, eating olives and sipping brandy, and soon the girl was gone and he said, "The funny thing is, there are apartments above these stores and this bar and all the time if you listen there's a child above here, she runs up and down what must be a long hall. I don't know why I'm so sure it's a girl because what she makes me think of is my son." Cholet lit a Gitanes and folded five dollars under the saucer on the table, nodded to the unshaven bartender and knotted his scarf *In the open doorway, her crossed arms under her breasts afloat in the lamplight, she said, "You know what's nice, most guys you meet the first time all they got is yack yack about themselves, right? but with you there's no yack yack." "And maybe I got nothing to say," I said, and she said, "Maybe so but that's why I wanted to take off my clothes for you earlier, like a little present, you know, because if sometimes you got nothing to say it doesn't mean you've got to lie and say something." Her hand out, touching, wistful, "And you got my number, right, if you want to call, okay, and you know what, I'm gonna get dressed, put on my pajamas and go to bed and have a real good sleep and thanks to you I feel real good," the door closing on the early morning, and out in the street a low-hanging mist, dong of the bell in the city hall and damp coolness soothing in the air, coming home, looking for some thread of light*

And a neon sign flashed down the street. "So there we were, you see," Cholet said, walking toward the stone gate, "surrounded by magazines, motors, private parts, and we're four old men dealing each other a hand in the middle of nowhere except for what we share, numbers, which make us closer than most men, numbers which are everything and nothing tattooed on the arms and last Friday we played till five in the morning and someone says it's the last pot like a last chance at life so all bets are doubled and he says you know what, let's play our numbers, like you see people in beer halls with dollar bills playing bullshit poker where they pair up the numbers on their bills, and we laugh a little but it seems like a good joke at so late an hour so we bet, the four of us, no cards necessary, but now our Chinese friend is left out and sour because he's got no chance to get even on his losses, and with each call there's more money and finally a big pot, so there we are facing each other, stiff in our white shirts still buttoned at the wrists, palms flat on the table, and the Chinese says okay show what you've got, but Jacob, he says there's some secrets you don't lie about and calls two pair, sixes and eights, but the way it works out, two pairs and Avrom's three threes are not good enough because I am three nines with a four and a five and so Avrom says, pushing all the money at me, smiling, Cholet, he says, you're a big winner, and I said yes, my heart beating, yes, and we all put on our coats like we always do at the door, laughing, and went home in the dark"

walking through the park, a misty night, street lamps in the elm leaves, with no lights on in the houses along the street except the front porch window from my floor lamp and there was nobody home in the empty house and in the dark, standing there in the bushes in the garden, I suddenly saw myself in the window, calm but hunched and my heart pounding, staring into my reflection, with her saying thanks for saying nothing and for making love to her, which was nothing but to her it was a lot, and wondering what was there to say to Cholet, except nothing.

Dark Laughter

IT WAS LATE AFTERNOON AND OVERCAST. THE LIGHT through the tinted ceiling glass of the sculpture hall made the large plaster maquettes by Henry Moore loom up like bones and socket holes hollowed by the wind. The security guard in the archway was watching two men who were walking arm in arm, taking their time. They looked like old friends, but they had met only that afternoon beside the reclining nude with the huge hips and the pellet head. They walked at an even pace, silent for a long while, a little shy but in step with each other. Every now and then they paused, looked at one of the huge white plaster casts, and once the older man said, "This is desert stuff, I've never seen the desert but the man who did this has got a desert wind inside his head." He smiled, kneading the palm of his hand, as if the soreness of an old wound were there. He seemed a little afraid of something, yet he was always smiling. "I'm dying," he said. "Some go quick, me, I'm going slowly, it's the human situation, that's all."

The younger man, who had narrow sloping shoulders, said, "You mean you're really sick?" The old man, his breath a little sour, holding the young man close to him, said, "Do I look sick to you? All a man needs is a pinch on the cheeks for a little colour," and he suddenly pinched the younger man playfully, laughing, saying, "My boy, my boy, what did you think when you saw me coming at you?"

"Nothing," he said warily, uncertain of what to make of this man who had started talking to him so intimately, as if he believed they shared something.

"Nothing? How can you think nothing when someone zeros in on you?"

"I don't know, I just thought, this guy's coming at me and I don't run from nothing. Never did, never will."

"Really now. So what do you do?"

"I own a wrecking lot."

"A what?"

"Cars. Trucks. A regular wrecking lot, you know, where old cars go."

"A wrecking lot. And you come here?" The older man smiled.

"Why not?" he said, a little wounded. "I feel at home, I like all the whiteness, like these things are the blown-up bones of birds."

"Birds? They look just like cow bones or horses to me."

"I only know about bird bones. I shoot birds."

The old man, rubbing the palm of his hand, stared at his open hand for a moment, and then pointed at a tall white totem sculpture. "It's like it's wearing a condom," he said.

"What?"

"It's like a plaster cast of a huge penis wearing a condom. By the way, where does a man like you shoot birds?"

"On the lot. Where else? Except I don't do it no more."

"Why not?"

"They learned, I guess, or maybe all those little skeletons lying around scare them away now." The guard stood with his eyes closed, half-asleep on his feet, and then, as if alert and on the watch, he opened his eyes and looked quickly around, sullen and unsmiling.

"So why?" the older man asked.

"Why what?"

"Why shoot birds, why would you want to shoot birds?"

"I didn't want to, I just did, that's all. I sit out there in the sun and there's nothing to do, except the sun's so nice on the hubcaps and fenders and such like, and the silence, I like that, and them caw-cawing crows and starlings just come and shit all over everything so I just take my time and shoot 'em dead because what I like best is silence, and when there's only the wind, and even better when there's no wind, except then you can always hear a fly, somewhere there's always a buzzing fly." He was talking at the top of his voice and the guard had taken three strides into the hall, hissing at them and flapping his arms. The older man, smiling, said, "What's your name?"

"Abel," the younger man said putting out his hand.

"Really, Abel?"

"My father's joke. My father's a joker who never laughs. His name's Adam so he called me Abel." The older man took his arm again and they began walking. The light had gone out of the skylight windows.

"So who's Cain?" the older man asked.

"Cain? What do I know? The whole world. Anyway, I got no brother. What's your name?"

"Luther."

"Luther what?"

"Luther Stahll."

"So what do you do, Luther Stahll, when you're not zeroing in on people in public galleries?"

"I was a cop. A few years ago."

"A cop. You get busted?"

"No, no. Nothing like that."

"You quit?"

"No. I just decided I didn't want to talk to anyone."

"Just like that?"

"Just about," he said, and tucked his head into his shoulder, an almost coy gesture, as if he were about to acknowledge some shameful secret about himself. But he was still smiling. "I was a swimmer, see, I mean a real police-games champion kind of swimmer, I could go longer and farther under water than anybody knew. I used to spend my lunch hours swimming under water, sometimes floating with my eyes closed like I was drifting toward I don't know what. I always had this sense in the silence, except it's not really a silence, you know, it's more like silent music would be if it could be silent, this feeling I was going somewhere, and one day I opened my eyes and I was staring into one of those big underwater round lights in the wall, a big eye of light swamping me, and I stared into it with my hands against the wall and I couldn't see anything and I had nothing to say so I just sat down and said nothing."

"For how long?"

"Nearly two years."

"My God. How could you stand it?"

"You're the one who's supposed to be so crazy for silence," Luther said.

"Yeah, but I gotta at least hear my own voice. I mean sometimes I get up in the morning and I say, it's a hell of a morning, and I feel good because I hear myself say it's a hell of a morning."

"Well, it's true, sometimes I laughed."

"Oh yeah. Well, that's something," Abel said, and stroked his long hair flat over his ears with the palms of his hands.

"It's everything," Luther insisted. "When I was alone, I'd sit on the front porch and I'd listen to myself laugh."

"What were you laughing at?"

"Not what. Who."

"Okay. Who?"

"God," he said, suddenly pinching Abel's cheek again. "See, a little pinch, look how healthy you look."

"Come on, lay off," Abel said, laughing shyly. "What the hell's God got to do with this?"

"Everything. I figure it's the one thing I learned being a cop. Try laughing at a cop when he's putting the arm on you and you know what he wants to do to you. He wants to kill you. But you laugh and there's nothing he can do. There's no law against laughter. It's your only revenge."

"You're not laughing," Abel said. "I don't hear you laughing."

"It's hard to laugh alone," Luther said, and stood for a moment alongside a sculpture that was so polished it was almost glazed and there were cords of white string bound around the white body. "You know what I think when I look at this, and this'll make you laugh, it reminds me of a plaster cast like you'd put on a broken arm, all wrapped like a butcher does in a meat market. I figure there's a big side of red, living, healing meat in there and someday they'll take the cast off."

"That don't make me laugh."

"It doesn't?"

"No."

Luther linked arms again and drew Abel close. "Listen," he said, "one day I went out walking for the first time in two years, and standing on the curb I got so fascinated by the cars I stepped out and got sideswiped, knocked down like I was dead as a doornail, and a priest from some church, he heard the noise and he came running." Luther had hold of Abel by the arm and he said, "I'm lying there like I'm under water, that's how I felt, half-hearing everything, except somehow I knew I was okay, and I opened my eyes and this priest is over me saying, 'Do you believe in God the Father, God the Son and God the Holy Ghost?' and I knew right there, absolutely, that he wouldn't laugh when I said to him, 'I'm dying and you ask me riddles.' "

Abel broke into sputtering, coughing laughter and Luther, as if he were relieved, as if a view he had of things had been confirmed, smacked his hands together, the smack echoing in the empty hall, and they were laughing together as he said, "I looked at that old priest and he had the strangest look in his eye, like some men do, you know, when they're down at the heels, half-broke and come from families that used to have money, he had that bewildered, regretful look, and I thought, my God, man, you're more alone than I ever was, and I just walked away laughing as hard as hell."

The security guard, hissing for silence, strode up to them and yelled, "Quiet. No disturbance is allowed."

"We're only laughing," Luther said.

"Then laugh quietly. This is a public place," the guard said sternly.

"I'm sick, my life's slipping away and you talk like that to me," Luther snorted, smiling as he led Abel by the elbow toward the archway, and he said, "Come on Abel, it's closing time anyway, we'll talk a little in the dark, it's dark out, you know, the sun's gone down." They walked out laughing quietly to themselves, side by side as if they were old friends.

Spring Water

THERE WAS AN OLD PRIEST WHO LED A QUIET LIFE. He said Mass every morning at the side altar of his church, and then read a mystery novel, had a light lunch, and went out walking. He was retired but he always made a few housecalls to talk to old friends, and though he had a special devotion to the Blessed Virgin, he didn't talk much about faith.

Though he was spry for a man in his late seventies, he distrusted people in a hurry. "Punctuality," he liked to say, "is for bored men. It's their special virtue. Myself, I'm always a little late saying Mass. That way, the latecomers end up on time." He was, however, precise about his dress, always wearing a well-pressed suit and the old dog collar, as he called it disarmingly, and then went on to say, "I've noticed the shirt and tie boys are the same guys who go in for sociology and statistics and think white socks are snappy with a black suit." He didn't like the way nuns dressed either. "I just don't see how dressing up in a drab sort of dress to get a little ankle on display makes them feel more of a woman in the world. Out in the world, yes. Women, no. But then what do I know about a woman's vanity, eh? I've only been listening to confessions for fifty years." He laughed, as if the joke were on him.

He liked walking, and talking while he walked. "It loosens up the body, don't you see, and loosens up the mind. You think in tune with yourself, except the streets are full of joggers these days, they're all over the place, and they're grim. You notice how grim they look? Men on the run always look grim, and sometimes I see them in bed, you know, with their wives, and not making love but just jogging in bed." He smiled, satisfied that he had touched on a small truth as he stood in the side aisle of St. Paul's Church on Power Street, shielding his eyes from the stained-glass light. It was the oldest parish in the city, but there were few parishioners now because the red brick Romanesque church was surrounded by small warehouses, and through the chancel window to the east there was only an expressway ramp and a police car with a radar gun at the foot of the ramp. He had said it was a beautiful church. "I was right, eh, except they've loused it up with the new altar. The old one was a beauty, and I'll tell you, the darnedest thing happened to me here years ago." He looked around quickly. The aisles were empty. "This man came in, head down, and he had a branch, a tree branch like a Y, you know. And he started marching up and down the aisles with the branch straight out from his belly, his elbows tucked into his ribs, and I recognized right away that he was witching for water. He was a diviner, and darned if that stick didn't whip down right at the altar rail, and he followed it on an angle to the station where Christ falls for the third time, and there must have been an

59

underground creek or something running right under there."

We were walking in late afternoon sunlight past secondhand stores, a cleaners and a shoe repair shop. "I spoke to him, you see, asked him what he was after, and he looked at me with this strange quizzical look, you know, as if he was sizing up whether he could trust me, and then he said to me like it was the most straightforward thing in the world, 'It's from my father's apple tree, he planted it the year I was born and it's better than the willow, they're just weeds,' and he said he only prayed where there was evidence, and I said evidence of what, and he smiled and said, 'Water, only where there's spring water, that's where I pray.'"

We had been walking along Mutual Street near the roller-skating rink, on our way to Diana Sweets where he always liked to have a dish of chocolate ice cream. I told him that was where I met my bookie, because he liked the ice cream, too. "Yes, yes," the old priest said. "Strange, how we're bound together and what it is that binds us. A little dish of ice cream, a little word in the dark." He said that over the years he had grown accustomed to listening to unsettling, disembodied voices in the dark confessional, voices coming to him through the grille, "Straight from the heart and uncluttered because they can't see me, of course, and one day a woman whispered, 'Do you think I've told the whole truth, Father?' and I said, 'Think of God as listening, an ear open to you, and He only wants to hear your voice, because it's the silence that kills God,' and that startled her, I'll say, so she says, 'Killed, Father?' which I naturally said was only a manner of speaking."

There was a middle-aged woman walking ahead, and she had thinning, almost candy-floss coloured hair. She wore a little pillbox hat with a veil. She was working a pocket calculator, pecking at it with her finger. "I hate flies," she said as we passed. "I hate the summer because I hate flies." The old priest nodded and said, "It'll all work out, give it time," as we turned a corner, facing the federal police headquarters, grey bunker towers of poured concrete, and a sour look came across his face. "I don't know, I don't know," he said. "Perhaps I make too much of these things, but a building's always been like a man's best suit to me. I've always been uneasy with men wearing bow ties and two-tone shoes. They tell me something about themselves, and when I look at a building like that, I try to take it just for what it is, what it's trying to tell me, and that's a building that doesn't trust anybody and I don't trust a person who doesn't trust anybody."

"A fine thing," I said, laughing, "for a priest to say about the police."

"Well, to tell you the truth, it's always been a weak spot of mine, the police. I can understand how a man can become a thief or a car salesman or just out-and-out shiftless, or even a priest, but I cannot understand why a man would want to be a policeman. A priest, after all, if he's any good at what he's doing and if he's not a dope, is engaged in forgiveness. But a policeman, if he's any good, is always putting the arm on a man. Punishment, plain and simple, and I'm no darned fool, there has to be punishment and people who do the punishing, but I just can't understand a man wanting to do that with his life. It's the wanting that puzzles me."

Inside Diana Sweets there was a line-up of women in singles and twos, shopping bags and bundles on each arm, and the counter itself was a little like a line-up, with women and a few lone men all sitting face forward, locked in their own thoughts, slowly twisting a napkin or examining the lipstick print on a cigarette. One woman in an olive-green cloth coat with a fox-fur neckpiece, the head of the fox with the dead glass eyes staring over her shoulder, began to shift and squirm when she saw the old priest, glancing at him, angry and sullen, some resentful memory suddenly alive inside her head, and as soon as we were seated at the counter she left, clutching her parcels. He didn't seem to notice.

"You know," he said, "we all reveal ourselves in strange ways, talking about the police I mean. There's this man Key, he's a retired cop, about seventy now, and there's always a piece in the newspaper about him, the way the old guy stays in such fantastic shape. I'm sure you've seen him. He passes me in the street all over town, a heel-and-toe walker, and the movement of the man, you see, fascinates me. Absolutely awkward, and yet with its own rhythm, up and down the streets he goes hooked on this heel-and-toe technique like a drug, except it's a discipline, because you can't make a mistake, you can't break stride, and I remember when I was a boy and this was a tiny little Methodist town, there were these huge heel-and-toe races, hundreds of men setting off like wind-up mechanical ducks, and this man Key's got that beaming, glazed look in his eyes like a man who's seen God, yet you know all he's seen is the wind in his face." He spooned the last of the dark chocolate ice cream from his silver dish. "I don't know why, but he seems to me like the perfect messenger sent out among us by the police."

A slightly dishevelled man in his thirties, sallow under the eyes and a stubble beard, sidled up between us and said familiarly to the priest, "It's been a long time, a long time, Father." Smiling weakly, yet with a certain sly self-assurance, he took a little square picture of Jesus from his pocket. It was a thick pebbled plastic picture of the Sacred Heart. It fitted the palm of his hand and he moved it back and forth between us, saying, "See, it never takes its eyes off you, the eyes move, I'm never out of the sight of the Lord, Father." He smiled again and the old priest, his hand coming out of his suit coat pocket, put a crumpled dollar bill into the young man's free hand. "Thank you, Father, thank you. God'll bless you, you'll see." He quickly went out the door.

"You know him before?" I said.

"No, not at all, not at all."

"You mean he panhandled you?"

"Well, you've got to admit, he was prepared, the moving eyes of the Lord is not bad," and he laughed so loudly and openly that some of the women along the counter looked at him, puzzled. He touched his paper napkin to his lips and then straightened the cuffs of his shirt, the little edge of white seeming to pick up all the light at his wrists, circles of light like the rim of white around his throat.

We paid the bill and went out onto Yonge Street. He stood staring at the new Eaton Centre, the big indoor shopping mall with walls of outside pipes and ducts, all exposed, and poured rough-cast concrete. "Funny," he said, "the way we've made a virtue of turning everything inside out. And Albert Street's gone, too. There used to be a small street there, where the subway entrance is. Years ago street preachers tried to out-holler each other on that corner, and I remember one fellah, I knew him pretty well, he had a chaw of tobacco in one side of his mouth and lectured on the Lord out of the other and his listeners had to leave a lane for him to spit, and he'd spit and yell, 'I spit on Satan,' knowing full well that tobacco was as evil as drink, but it didn't seem to matter to him. He was a baseball player, you see. Chewed tobacco all the time."

We continued up Yonge Street, taking our time. Young pasty-faced girls, with coats pulled across their breasts under their crossed arms, hurried from strip bar to strip bar. He saw them but said nothing. "Have you ever thought about baseball?" he asked. "You played ball, didn't you?"

"What do you mean think about it?"

"Well, it's not a team sport, you know."

"It's not?"

"No, no, not at all," and he smiled, bemused, "nothing's ever what it appears. It's a one-on-one game, you see. Each pitch the pitcher throws, it's a battle between two men, and then the batter hits the ball and suddenly he's a runner trying to outrun the shortstop's throwing arm. It's all like that, separate moments, one to one, like a man with his God. A meditative game, you see. Haven't you noticed how many priests are always at ball games, the leisurely time between each play for speculation, all the players' percentages like so much counting of angels on the heads of pins? It's wonderful, played so wide open and yet with its own logic. And if you want to carry the point, the owners, they're conservative to the core, they're all cardinals, the Curia, you see, not my cup of tea at all, the high moral tone of the man in charge."

The afternoon light was gone. In the doorway of a closed clothing store, two young street players were singing, one playing a guitar and the other skipping and twirling a silver-painted rope like it was a big noose, keeping to the beat, doing crossovers and triple time steps. They seemed furtive and afraid back in the shadows, as if ready to move on, because the police always rousted street singers out of the doorways. Businessmen said they were bad for business. But the old priest stopped and listened, still talking quietly. "And then, you see, what's beautiful about baseball is every now and then a guy like this man Fidrych comes along, the kid pitcher for Detroit, you know, and he talks to the ball and talks to the grass and gets down and eats the dirt on the pitcher's mound, a holy magic fool with a fast ball no one can hit, and nothing seizes the mind like a holy fool, like a saint. You see, he does everything all wrong and he's wacky but he's got the special touch."

He stood listening to the boys, smiling broadly, and gave a clap of his hands, pleased with them and a little excited by his own sense of things, and then he stepped forward and bent down in front of the boys, over the black felt hat in the doorway, and dropped in a dollar. "Very good, boys," he said. "Thank you, Father," the silver-rope dancer called out, and as the old priest walked away he said, "A silver rope, now that's good, I've never seen that before, dancing in and out of a rope, doing time steps."

The sun was going down and the neon lights were all flashing. It was suddenly cool and I turned up my coat collar and said, "I don't get it."

"Get what?"

"You, the way you light up with that panhandler, with those kids."

"Oh," he said, suddenly a little shy. Then he touched me lightly on the sleeve and said, "Spring water, see. Only where there's spring water."

The Muscle

LIVIO WAS LATE FOR SCHOOL BECAUSE OF THE morning walk he'd taken with his father, a long walk, and in front of Settimio's Café where there were chrome coffee machines in the window, his father had insisted that they sit down at one of the small arborite tables and have a thimble-cup of good strong espresso, and he'd smiled and patted Livio's hand as if it were the old days of bleaching morning sunlight in the village. Then they had hurried along the street to the dowdy red brick school and at the door he'd said, "Livio, you listen, always listen to the teacher."

His father had been a stonemason in the hills outside Taormina, and his father loved stone, the way it captured light and held it, he said, like life itself, speckled with colour, and yet it could be a dead weight almost as heavy as a dead body, except stones never sleep, he said, though the real secret of stone like the stone he'd cut for the village fountain was when you held it to your ear. If you listened hard you could hear water, water locked in the stone, and Livio always wondered why the village men sat hunched against the stone with their legs stretched out, never listening, not even to each other, as they laughed and joked and got quietly drunk on black wine in the early evening.

When Livio got to the classroom he hung back at the door, not because he was a little late but because Mr. Beale the history teacher always made him feel small and unimportant, made him feel like a stranger who could never belong in this new world. Yet it consoled him to know that all the students felt unimportant when Mr. Beale was teaching.

He was talking about Rome. He was a tall and easygoing man with a confident air who collected ancient glass bottles, and he sometimes brought them to class so he could show the students how all the impurities in the once clear glass had caused beautiful lace-like discolourations. He liked to amble back and forth in his tweed suit, talking in a rambling, authoritative way about history, and sometimes he would open his long arms wide as if he were offering his students all the wisdom in the world.

Livio hoped he could sneak into the room without Mr. Beale noticing. He never wanted Mr. Beale to notice him again because the last time Livio was late Mr. Beale had said sarcastically, "Where did you come from?" as if he had never seen him before. "You don't belong here, do you? Ah, you do, you do, I do believe that's true," and all the students had laughed, and later, between classes, they had called out, "Where you from, Livio boy?"

But he hesitated too long at the door and Mr. Beale saw him and cried, "Come in, come in, you're among friends," and someone at the back of the room snickered as Livio sat down, hunched forward, listening to Mr. Beale who was suddenly standing in the light in front of the big window, opening his arms.

"Livio, you should know about this, I bet you know all about Rome and Carthage, yes? So, the great question is did the Romans make a mistake, was it a mistake to wipe out Carthage?"

Livio looked up, wondering, a little wide-eyed, shaking his head.

"Carthage," Mr. Beale repeated dryly.

"Yes," Livio said.

"*Delenda est Carthago,*" Mr. Beale said.

"Yes."

"Was it a mistake, eh? Was it in their own interest to kill off their enemy for ever?"

"No, Carthage no mistake" Livio said, smiling.

"Wrong," Mr. Beale said, turning away. "These things always seem so simple, but life's complex, boys," and he turned back to Livio for a moment with a wan smile and then went on to explain that the Romans should have worked out a deal with the Carthaginians in the same way the Americans had come to terms with Germany after the war. "Because you can't get blood out of a stone. You've got to get your enemy in debt to you, make them thankful partners, because you can't feed off yourself surrounded by people entirely alien to you, which is what Rome ended up doing, and you won't find that in your books," he said. The class was over. He looked pleased with himself.

He put these difficult questions to Livio every day and sometimes Livio stared and said nothing, not sure what was going on. One day Mr. Beale, throwing open his arms, said, "Livio, you pay attention, always you listen, you gotta to listen," and the boys broke into loud laughter. Mr. Beale smiled and patted one of the laughing boys on the back as he walked to the blackboard.

Livio sat rubbing his knuckles, but then he thought about his father who was no longer a stonemason, but only a bricklayer uprooted from a village that had been bombed by the Americans during the war and then left behind broken and empty, and now he was living with his wife and son in a damp basement flat, laying bricks and working like a day labourer and never complaining. When Mr. Beale went by and tapped Livio on the shoulder, saying, "You do well Livio, you get better every day," he sat locked in silence, confused and angry, remembering a little mute boy everyone in the village had made fun of, and his father had told him that there were voices inside the boy, deep inside, and all he had to do was open up the boy's mouth and put his ear as close as he could and he'd hear them, he'd hear strange old grandfathers whispering, and one day Livio had pried the frightened boy's mouth open, staring down into the dark gaping hole that smelled so sour he had turned away, surprised as the boy broke into tears, his mouth hanging open, and Livio, sitting very straight in his seat, felt like crying, afraid that Mr. Beale might come and force open his mouth. Closing his eyes, Livio drifted off into a dream of village evenings and how he used to amuse his father and the men around the fountain with the little trick muscle in his wrist.

One afternoon Livio rolled up his sleeve and felt the two little cords that ran down his right wrist, and then he put a quarter on the cords, clenching his right fist, slowly turning his wrist. The cords tensed and then a small muscle popped up, the coin flipped over on its head and landed perfectly on his wrist. Livio smiled. The boy sitting behind Livio poked him and said, "Hey, do that again." Livio shook his head. "Come on, I want to see that again."

Livio put the coin on the cords, clenched his fist and turned his wrist and the boy leaned forward. Livio, suddenly at ease, laughed with the boy as the coin flipped over.

"What's going on there?"

Livio slumped down in his seat, but the boy leaned into the aisle and said, "Livio has a trick, sir."

"Livio has a trick. What kind of trick?"

Mr. Beale, buttoning his suit coat, came to their seats. "Let's see your trick, Livio."

Livio shook his head.

"Come on, we your friends, we gotta see everything you canna do." Mr. Beale turned to the class. "Don't we class?"

The boys shouted yes and the boy behind Livio pushed him. "Go on, show them."

Livio looked up and saw Mr. Beale, aloof, stroking his neck, the light on his narrow face from the big window, and Mr. Beale said softly, almost soothingly, "You show us your little trick, eh, Livio."

Livio put the coin on his wrist. All the boys were watching him. The muscle popped up and the coin flipped over. The class was silent and then someone called out, "Do it again."

Livio quickly put the coin back on his wrist, but Mr. Beale said no to Livio and then wheeled on the class with a wave of his arms. "We don't a turn thisa room into a circus." But there was no laughter. "We can't have this in the middle of class," he said sternly. "We've got work to do."

"But you said you wanted to see it," a boy cried.

Mr. Beale shrugged, as if what had happened was of no consequence because they were all friends and it was over, but Livio suddenly stood up and thrust the coin out at the teacher, who, startled, waved Livio aside, but Livio held out the coin to him again.

"You want me to try your little trick?"

Livio nodded and sat down.

"You think no one else can do your little trick?"

Mr. Beale rolled up his sleeve and put the coin on his wrist. Clenching his fist, he twisted his wrist back and forth, yet the coin stayed still. He flushed, little blotches of red breaking out in his cheeks as he stood staring at the profile of the Queen on the coin, his long arm extended, his hand white. The class began to laugh. Humiliated by the laughter, he tossed the coin into Livio's lap and went back to his desk, picking up a book and then putting it down. He began to write all the dates of Caesar's conquests on the blackboard and he told them to memorize the dates.

When class was over the boys gathered around Livio. The tallest, Luther Such, who was muscular but wore thick glasses, smacked him on the back and asked him to do that trick again. Livio shuffled as if he were too shy. Mr. Beale, trying to be friendly and part of the good feeling, called out, "You don't want to forget the football game, boys," but no one paid any attention. Livio saw the teacher lift his arm as if to speak, but the boys were all laughing and Mr. Beale sat down. The room cleared and Livio and the teacher were alone.

With a loose smile on his face Mr. Beale stood up awkwardly as if wanting to be bigger than Livio. Feeling uncertain for a moment, Livio finally looked up, smiling. "My English pretty good, eh?" he said helpfully. "I think I do pretty good."

"Very well, Livio, you've done very well."

"I think it's so."

Livio didn't know what to do. There was a button missing on the teacher's suit coat sleeve, and Mr. Beale stood twisting the loose nub of thread. He seemed to be waiting for some snide little word from Livio, sure that it was coming, but then Livio suddenly reached out and took Mr. Beale's hand. His own blue wide-open eyes had a vulnerable look, yet his grip on Mr. Beale's hand was firm. "I don't hold no hard feelings, Mr. Teacher," he said. "You neither, I think, eh?"

"No, no. Of course not, Livio," he said stiffly, as if sure he was being mocked in some new way by a boy who deeply disliked him.

"Sir, it's only a trick," Livio said, fumbling for the right words. "I practise. You practise, too, sir, eh?" and he took the coin out of his pocket and put it in Mr. Beale's hand, the one he was holding. "Take it, sir. Friends now, eh?"

"Well, now, see here ..." Mr. Beale began, his face suddenly flushing again, and because of the way Mr. Beale was staring at him Livio felt uneasy. Mr. Beale looked lonely and disappointed, a look Livio had seen in the eyes of men slouched around his father's fountain, and he wondered if the teacher knew that stones never sleep and sometimes are heavy because they're full of stone seeds.

"Livio," Mr. Beale began, and then his hand tightened on Livio's, the grip suddenly so tight it was painful. "Thank you. Thank you very much," he said. Looking at the coin he said quickly, "Yes, Livio, I'll really hold on to this," as if he had hold of his self-respect again.

The Cohen in Cowan

COWAN'S MY NAME AND IN CASE YOU DON'T KNOW Cowan's cut down from Cohen 'cause Cohen meant you were a king but I'm a Cowan, which lets you know right away where I stand, which is on my own two feet, and where else, 'cause I used to be Jewish but now I'm very successful, otherwise would I have a black car like a regular mayor or a mortician if I wasn't successful? But mostly I know I'm okay 'cause I get no secret sweats in the night though I got a lot on my mind and sometimes the pressure is a cooker like you wouldn't believe, but I don't owe no one in this whole world for what I got, which is to say my company from day one was a moneymaker I thought up in the shower room at the Y and where the idea came from is one night I'm watching the Oscar awards and this song *You Light Up My Life*, which I always thought was a Flick-Your-Bic commercial, wins 'cause it turns out it's a song about God but what I'm looking for's got nothing to do with God but only this company I put together as a dodge for tax purposes, out near the old cemetery and it has got to look legit. So in the shower after playing basketball I think to myself I'll get into the T-shirt business with T-shirts from Taiwan, to which if you send me a photo I'll put your face dead centre between your tits for all the world to see, which is better than all these Day-Glo slogans 'cause it's you yourself, which is when I get the company name when I hear myself saying U-yourself, and that's where we all live 'cause nothing counts like old Number One, which doesn't mean I don't have a Number Two, namely my wife who loves me a lot, but the fact is, I'm at my best alone in the Y and so standing the next day in the shower room I think, why not lampshades with your face on your own lampshade, which my wife says is a little weird for a Jew but I say forget the Jewish problem and let the light that lights up your room light up your face. That's what we all want, to look good in a good light, and pretty soon there's so many orders I know I'm on to a lucky streak, and sure enough one afternoon I'm out walking past one of these religious stores with prayer books and those beads and I stop dead in my tracks. I can feel for sure somebody's got their eye on me and pretty soon I figure it out, it's this 3-D holy picture with the big heart bleeding and my wife she says she's worried about lampshades being in bad taste, and there I am looking at this dripping heart with a red light bulb in it, which to me is really sick, but bleeding hearts are not my business except the world's full of bleeding hearts, but these big mooning eyes no matter where I move, they follow me 'cause of the way they're printed in this pebbly plastic and bam like a light it hits me. Put U-yourself In The Picture With A Frame Of Simulated Walnut. I tell you this is terrific like you can't believe 'cause there's nothing people like better than the look of themselves on the wall keeping an eye on everything and you think T-shirts are big, I'm getting photographs from the end of the earth and I'm making big bucks, which suits me fine except suddenly I'm a businessman tied to an accountant instead of a tax dodge, and I don't want to be a businessman like that 'cause actually though I'm very respectable you see I'm a bookie.

But even more than being a bookie I like playing basketball, but mostly by myself 'cause it's not that I can't keep up with the boys, being only thirty-six and I got what my wife calls a little pleasure-pillow paunch, but I don't like to complicate my life with too many other people who only make demands and one demand leads to another. So I like being alone bouncing a ball on Sunday mornings at the Y when there's nobody on the floor and usually there's only one old guy out that early jogging around the upstairs track like he's chasing his own shadow. He don't pay attention to me and I don't pay attention to him but we quit around the same time 'cause other guys are now on the floor and B-ball is really only terrific when you're by yourself 'cause when you're alone you can get this feather touch in the fingers, your whole body light like weightless, and you take off and float with the ball, looping it up off the backboard and bam it goes swish. That's as close to perfect perfection as you're gonna get, knowing you're totally in tune between yourself and the ball, and before you even take a look you see it happen before it happens, which my wife she tells me is almost mystical or musical, I forget the way she says I talk about it, but it's true. The only time I felt close to totally happy is the one or two times I got that feather touch in my fingers, like the little flutter I feel sometimes from my wife except my wife and me, who everybody says we were made for each other in heaven, one week we nearly come apart at the seams and for Christsake can you believe it, all over a lousy Christmas tree.

Which was not because I'm Jewish but the way I remember being Jewish, which in some ways is worse than being Jewish because it's always in the back of your mind and by and large what you remember is what you are which is why I figure that what a person wants to forget should take care of itself, except there are some things you can't do nothing about and for me it's the smells I smell, and comes Christmas time and I see Christmas trees what I think of is *shiksas*, and what I thought about *shiksas* when I was a boy was pork, and when I think of pork I get queasy 'cause unclean's unclean, which don't make much sense 'cause actually I like eating great big *goyish* hams with pineapple rings. But what can I do about what I smell in my head whether it smells that way or not, so when my wife says she wants a Christmas tree so my two little daughters can open up their presents like regular kids, and I say they're not regular kids, she says why not, and I say 'cause they're nothing the way everyone else is something, and she says that don't make no sense 'cause nobody's anything these days so what's the difference and what do I care, and I tell her I care and she says not about them and then I'm suddenly screaming pork and she looks at me for the first time in our lives like I'm crazy, which I suddenly feel I am, standing there in the kitchen going pork pork, but there's no way I'm gonna be the first person who's Jewish or not in my family who has a Christmas tree in his house. For all I know what she wants is a star up on top like I'm supposed to be one of the three wise men wishing I knew which way to turn, which is the trouble with wise guys who got all the answers for everybody but themselves, 'cause they got stars in their eyes which I don't.

Nonetheless now I'm in the dark with my wife who is a looker and she's cut me off with absolutely no nookie no way and let's face it, I'm a very sexy person who doesn't like lying awake in the dark, so I'm sitting up downstairs half the night trying to figure out what's going on, staring at the turned-off TV tube staring back at me like I'm nuts, and there's my own face on the lampshade over the piano all lit up and so I turn on the matching lamp on the mantelpiece and there's my wife all dolled up like Snow White staring at me smiling in the lampshade and between us on the wall my little girls are hanging in their plastic pictures looking at me no matter where I move like the world's coming to an end over this lousy tree. I can't stand it 'cause my wife says why should people who're nothing sit around with nothing to do, especially when we don't care what's what with anyone, except I know we care 'cause we're screaming at each other the whole time, and I tell her we're making something outa nothing 'cause already I'm sleeping on the sofa and what's even worse everything's out of whack with me being a bookie 'cause now I'm losing.

And I want you to know bookies don't lose unless something is really wrong 'cause betting is the way I see things hanging together in a framework, and when I used to bet myself I was always looking for the sign when I couldn't do nothing wrong no matter how I played it, like the hand of God was with me, and lots of times I got the sign, but even when you believe you're so right you win big, you know you always got to end up losing, like no matter how successful we are we know we all got to die, so one day I can see the only winner is whoever's collecting the bets 'cause the world's full of losers, so I got into being a bookie and right away I'm on the side of the angels and getting rich. Except now I'm sleeping on the sofa and every *putz* in town is picking winners so I'm going broke, and I figure it's all 'cause of that tree, so I'm driving home in a snowstorm the day before Christmas and there's this lot full of scruffy trees for fifteen bucks each, which is outrageous, but I buy one anyway 'cause I'm suddenly so excited like I haven't been for a long time. I can't wait to see my wife's face light up like I flicked her Bic when she sees this tree.

So what I see as soon as I say hello is my wife standing with her arms crossed in the living room in front of a great big tree. It's all dripping with tinsel and tiny lights and there's a lopsided star up on top and my kids are sitting cross-legged in the corner looking scared but she's staring at my tree and I'm staring at her tree and all of a sudden we both start laughing ourselves to death, thank God, 'cause maybe I would've killed her for doing that to me if I hadn't done it to myself. So after we stop laughing she says I can't just throw my tree away so maybe I should call the cathedral but I say what do I know about cathedrals, and she says that's exactly their business, looking after poor people who need a tree, but now I think I'm losing my mind when I call the cathedral and this priest is talking very softly to me saying yes, and what a blessing and don't I know there's plenty of families who not only don't have trees but they don't have turkeys either, and like I'm going crazy I whisper back to him, how about I buy them a nice big ham. But he laughs real quiet like we're sharing some secret and says a turkey'll do just fine and he's very touched, and I tell him no I'm the one that's touched, right in the head, and he gives me this little chuckle again saying the Lord really does work in wondrous ways.

The only way I feel is like I'm bleeding to death when two guys from the church show up all smiles, and when I give them the cheque for the turkey the guy with the peak cap says it's a fine tree you have for yourself there Mr. Cowan and a fine Christian thing you do, and I'm smiling like my face is falling apart at the seams. Suddenly I want to yell Cohen you creep, I'm Cohen, but my wife's giving me her little flutter touch on the small of my back and I get this loose feeling like everything's okay and pretty soon me and my wife are standing in the doorway like a couple of loonies saying Merry Christmas to these two guys carrying the tree to their pickup truck. Later we lie around with the kids gone to bed listening for reindeer on the roof and I say maybe I should come down the chimney and my wife says chimneys are a very bad joke for a Jew but I tell her for Christsake cut it out 'cause I'm already feeling a little lost like it is, lying there looking out the window at the really shining stars I never really saw like that before.

In the morning I can't believe it 'cause I'm lying there in this terrific sleep when the phone rings beside the bed, and I hear giggling downstairs that makes me think of summer and the water sprinkler on the lawn, but this voice is saying in my ear he wants to thank me especially Mr. Cowan for my kindness, and I don't know who the hell he is so I say he's very welcome but then I realize he's talking about how tickled he is by my tree and my turkey. He says he took a chance looking up my name in the book because there's got to be only one Adrian H. Cowan, which I tell him is true, and he says he can believe it and sounds so warm and pleased I'm suddenly sitting up smiling and puffing the pillows, asking him how it all looks and he's talking terrific, until he says so why not drop over Mr. Cowan and take a look 'cause it'd be a real pleasure to meet a man like me, which I say likewise I'm sure and I will and I hang up and think oh my God, I'm gonna hang myself, 'cause I can't believe how I've done this to myself, telling this poor guy I'm gonna come around and stand in his kitchen and stare at his turkey and tree, which is really my tree, and so I go downstairs and this I can't believe either. The whole room is littered up with paper and my little girls are laughing and yelling Daddy Daddy, giving me gifts, and I can't stand it 'cause for them I got no gifts, but my wife says the whole day's this wonderful gift from me and what a wonderful man I am, and like she's at last telling me the biggest secret of her life she says she's already made a plum pudding.

Which is what happens when you give a little you get a lot and I'm gone all the way from pork to plum pudding, so all of a sudden I feel like I'm sitting in a corner with my thumb in someone else's life and I really pulled out a plum, except this is no plum, this is painful, 'cause she says she's got Irish coffees and plum pudding at eleven o'clock in the morning for neighbours who don't care about Jewish, and why, I want to know, is this happening to me in my own house, that everybody is so happy when all I want is nothing except a little piece of the action and no talking to smooth-talking priests. So I say thank you very much, I don't want to be a spoilsport, but I'm going to the Y while it's still early and play a little B-ball by myself. My wife, she taps me on the cheek like it's my *tuchis* and says she understands, smiling, when I know she don't understand at all, and I tell her for the last time that this is the way I am, which is nothing, and kiss her hard 'cause I'm holding her so hard I feel I'm gonna cry, and even when I'm in my big black car I feel I'm gonna cry, driving like I got nothing but time through the streets that are so empty.

And all I can think of is going to see this guy with my tree, which is his fault 'cause I didn't call him, he called me, and actually he lives down close to where my father lived, which is not such a bad place except I haven't been there for years, and when I'm driving down the street I feel a little weird, like I'm moving back into my father's life which is my life, and suddenly I wish I had a son looking for himself in me the way I could look for me in my father if I wanted to, even though my father's dead twenty years, but still I got his old gabardine coat somewhere in a box with his long underwear that he died in when he fell down in the slush in the street and some cop said to me like I was someone else's son, the old *sheeny*'s dead, which made me want to kill him when I was a little boy but instead I grew up and got smart and changed my name to Cowan so my kids don't get that kinda crap in case I die in the street.

Then before I know it I'm getting out of my car facing this number 48 like the guy on the phone said, and I mean this house is so bad it's nothing like my father ever knew, 'cause the verandah's slipping left while the house is leaning right, and I'm standing there in the street in my own very terrific suede coat with the fox-fur collar and bam, it hits me like I can see this guy's face go out like a light. No matter how much he says he wants to thank me personally there's no way he'd like me looking down at his family beaming up at me and all of a sudden I feel this terrific sadness like I just lost my whole childhood, 'cause I hear myself humming I'm the king of the castle and you're the dirty rascal, and I know if I go in there, then there's no way I can come out clean, so I feel kinda left out like I'm trapped between what I done and what I can't do so that almost without thinking I lifted my hand like I was saying goodbye, and it was only when I was back driving alone in the car that I saw my hand in the air like it was a blessing the way my father used to bless me.

And I want you to know it's not a question of counting blessings, but I can't remember blessing anybody, not even my own kids, which makes me feel even a little more sad but when I'm in the locker room putting on my running shoes I know I'm all wound up and alive inside like I can't wait to get on the floor and then I find the gym is totally empty with not even the old guy running around the track, like he knew this morning I needed to be alone absolutely, and everything I do with the ball feels loose and I'm doing lay-ups real easy and I get this weird feeling that whatever I want is right there at my finger tips. I start dropping in shots from fifteen feet and I suddenly start doing backhanders and scoops and crossovers and double pumps. I can't miss like I'm unconscious I'm so good, and then I drop this long looping hook shot like a rainbow from almost centre court, which I know before I even let it go it's perfect, and for a minute I want to cry again and I want the guy with my tree to be there sitting maybe in a folding chair with his turkey in his arms seeing this, 'cause suddenly I got the conviction that we're connected though I never seen him and he's never seen me, but somehow I know I got the touch like it was given to me maybe in the street when I had my hand in the air, which is what my father always used to do when he'd just put his hand in the air over my head and say nothing like he was real peaceful, and so I'm thinking about this guy like he's there all peaceful with his face lit up, and suddenly I'm standing at centre court doing something I could never do before, which is get the ball spinning on my finger tip like it is the whole world and I feel this terrific astonishment which I can't explain, I'm so surprised at being alive let alone I should have this special touch, which for once in my life I really know I got, 'cause for once I did what I didn't intend to do, which was leave the guy alone with whatever happiness he got from what I gave him, and my only regret was he couldn't call me by my real name which is Cohen 'cause now my name is Cowan, which lets you know right away where I stand except standing there at centre court I didn't feel that I was me at all 'cause I don't exactly know who I am but now I know I'm not nothing.

The Black Queen

HUGHES AND MCCRAE WERE FASTIDIOUS MEN WHO took pride in their old colonial house, the clean simple lines and stucco walls and the painted pale blue picket fence. They were surrounded by houses converted into small warehouses, trucking yards where houses had been torn down, and along the street, a school filled with foreign children, but they didn't mind. It gave them an embattled sense of holding on to something important, a tattered remnant of good taste in an area of waste overrun by rootless olive-skinned children.

McCrae wore his hair a little too long now that he was going grey, and while Hughes with his clipped moustache seemed to be a serious man intent only on his work, which was costume design, McCrae wore Cuban heels and lacquered his nails. When they'd met ten years ago Hughes had said, "You keep walking around like that and you'll need a body to keep you from getting poked in the eye." McCrae did all the cooking and drove the car.

But they were not getting along these days. Hughes blamed his bursitis but they were both silently unsettled by how old they had suddenly become, how loose in the thighs, and their feet, when they were showering in the morning, seemed bonier, the toes longer, the nails yellow and hard, and what they wanted was tenderness, to be able to yield almost tearfully, full of a pity for themselves that would not be belittled or laughed at, and when they stood alone in their separate bedrooms they wanted that tenderness from each other, but when they were having their bedtime tea in the kitchen, as they had done for years using lovely green and white Limoges cups, if one touched the other's hand then suddenly they both withdrew into an unspoken, smiling aloofness, as if some line of privacy had been crossed. Neither could bear their thinning wrists and the little pouches of darkening flesh under the chin. They spoke of being with younger people and even joked slyly about bringing a young man home, but that seemed such a betrayal of everything that they had believed had set them apart from others, everything they believed had kept them together, that they sulked and nettled away at each other, and though nothing had apparently changed in their lives, they were always on edge, Hughes more than McCrae.

One of their pleasures was collecting stamps, rare and mint-perfect, with no creases or smudges on the gum. Their collection, carefully mounted in a leatherbound blue book with seven little plastic windows per page, was worth several thousand dollars. They had passed many pleasant evenings together on the Directoire settee arranging the old ochre- and carmine-coloured stamps. They agreed there was something almost sensual about holding a perfectly preserved piece of the past, unsullied, as if everything didn't have to change, didn't have to end up swamped by decline and decay. They disapproved of the new stamps and dismissed them as crude and wouldn't have them in their book. The pages for the recent years remained empty and they liked that; the emptiness was their statement about themselves and their values, and Hughes, holding a stamp up into the light between his tweezers, would say, "None of that rough trade for us."

One afternoon they went down to the philatelic shops around Adelaide and Richmond streets and saw a stamp they had been after for a long time, a large and elegant black stamp of Queen Victoria in her widow's weeds. It was rare and expensive, a dead-letter stamp from the turn of the century. They stood side by side over the glass counter-case, admiring it, their hands spread on the glass, but when McCrae, the overhead fluorescent light catching his lacquered nails, said, "Well, I certainly would like that little black sweetheart," the owner, who had sold stamps to them for several years, looked up and smirked, and Hughes suddenly snorted, "You old queen, I mean why don't you just quit wearing those goddamn Cuban heels, eh? I mean why not?" He walked out leaving McCrae embarrassed and hurt and when the owner said, "So what was wrong?" McCrae cried, "Screw you," and strutted out.

Through the rest of the week they were deferential around the house, offering each other every consideration, trying to avoid any squabble before Mother's Day at the end of the week when they were going to hold their annual supper for friends, three other male couples. Over the years it had always been an elegant, slightly mocking evening that often ended bitter-sweetly and left them feeling close, comforting each other.

McCrae, wearing a white linen shirt with starch in the cuffs and mother-of-pearl cuff links, worked all Sunday afternoon in the kitchen and through the window he could see the crab-apple tree in bloom and he thought how in previous years he would have begun planning to put down some jelly in the old pressed glass jars they kept in the cellar, but instead, head down, he went on stuffing and tying the pork loin roast. Then in the early evening he heard Hughes at the door, and there was laughter from the front room and someone cried out, "What do you do with an elephant who has three balls on him...you don't know, silly, well you walk him and pitch to the giraffe," and there were howls of laughter and the clinking of glasses. It had been the same every year, eight men sitting down to a fine supper with expensive wines, the table set with their best silver under the antique carved wooden candelabra.

Having prepared all the raw vegetables, the cauliflower and carrots, the avocados and finger-sized miniature corns-on-the-cob, and placed porcelain bowls of homemade dip in the centre of a pewter tray, McCrae stared at his reflection for a moment in the window over the kitchen sink and then he took a plastic slipcase out of the knives-and-forks drawer. The case contained the dead-letter stamp. He licked it all over and pasted it on his forehead and then slipped on the jacket of his charcoal-brown crushed velvet suit, took hold of the tray, and stepped out into the front room.

The other men, sitting in a circle around the coffee

table, looked up and one of them giggled. Hughes cried, "Oh my God." McCrae, as if nothing were the matter, said, "My dears, time for the crudités." He was in his silk stocking feet, and as he passed the tray he winked at Hughes who sat staring at the black queen.

All the Lonely People

I

THEY MET AT AN INUIT SCULPTURE GALLERY. SHE started talking to him as if they were casual old friends. Her name was Helen. As they walked around a whalebone bird with two heads he said, "Don't you see, they were after the spirit already there inside the bone. What emerges is in the bones." When they went for coffee she sat very straight in her chair and several times she opened her pocket mirror and looked at herself, touching her lipstick with her little finger, as if she were never sure of herself, but after their first week together, meeting in the late afternoons at his small bookshop and walking in the speckled light of the heavily treed parks close by her big old family home, she suddenly disappeared without warning, travelling alone, phoning first from Boston and then from Palm Springs where she had old school friends. "Don't worry about me, Arthur," she said. "The one thing I know how to do is look after myself." She had been married to a scholar, a specialist in Anglo-Saxon riddles, "And he said I made him feel like he'd done something wrong. He was quite unfair, saying that. We just didn't agree any more." Her mother and father were dead and she lived alone in her family home.

One afternoon she came and sat in Arthur's long narrow bookshop, staring at the walls lined with books, some of them old and rare and locked behind glass doors. "It's a little like a tunnel in here," she said, smiling, but she didn't ask to see anything and didn't open a book, and later, while they were in the upstairs sitting room of her house listening to Ravel, she said, "Does it bother you that we haven't made love?"

"No," he said, taking her hand.

"I think we should make love," she said. "I've chilled some white wine."

Her large bedroom at the back of the house was filled with light. There was a polar-bear skin on the floor and panel mirrors on the wall beside the brass bed. "Does it embarrass you?" she asked.

"Why should it?" he said shyly.

Later, when they were resting in bed, she said, "You know, my husband made up a riddle about me."

"What was it?" Arthur asked.

"I don't know. It was in Anglo-Saxon. No one knows Anglo-Saxon. Anyway, was I good?"

"Yes," he said. She had been silent while they made love, watching herself in the mirror.

"What else could you say?" She closed her eyes, touching the inside of her thighs.

"I could say no."

"No you couldn't," she said, pulling the sheet up to her breasts which were smaller than he had thought. "What do you think about women's lib?"

"I don't think about it at all."

"I think it's awful. What was quiet desperation is now noisy desperation. By the way, could I have a photograph of you, a nice one?"

"Sure," he said, pleased.

"Did you look?" she said, sipping her wine.

"Once."

"I love to look. Sometimes I feel I'm watching someone who's not me with her legs up in the air."

She smoothed her hair away from her face.

"What did you see?" she said.

"I don't know."

"Come on. Don't be shy."

"You've got just that little bit of blonde hair between your legs, like no hair at all."

"No, I mean in the mirror."

"I was surprised at how big I looked, when I was in you."

The following week, she said she didn't want to make love. "I could tell you I have the curse," she said, "but the truth is I want us to keep calm before we make love again." She led him through the house, opening up small formal sitting rooms, the breakfast room and the library, and china cabinets filled with figurines and albums that had pages of photographs of her father. "I don't use most of the rooms but I like to keep them like they look as if they're lived in." She had become a collector of things and one night she got undressed slowly at the bottom of the stairs so he could watch her walk up the stairs wearing black lace underwear and a black garter belt. She said she'd bought them at an auction in Palm Springs because they had belonged to Aimee Semple McPherson. Then, in the bedroom, she made love to him, telling him to stand with his back to the mirrors. He felt a warm unsettling surge, as if he could throttle her as he stood with his hands on her shoulders near her neck, and he wanted to see her face but he could only see the flood of her auburn hair and the small of her back and her buttocks, and he tried to find her in the mirror but he could see nothing.

They lay on the bed listening to music and she said, "Didn't your father ever tell you anything? I mean, we all remember something our fathers told us after they're dead."

"Sure."

"What?"

"Always get a good lawyer."

"Why in the world would he say that?" she said, laughing.

"He was an honest man who liked life."

"So?"

"So, he was foolish about himself but not about other men."

"Anything else?"

"Anything else what?"

"Did he tell you anything else?"

"Always keep a clear head."

"What did that mean?"

"He was a salesman and he always warned me to watch out for fast talkers. Keep a clear head and don't get fooled, he used to say."

"That was all?"

"Just about."

"What else?"

"You won't like it."

"Maybe I will, maybe I won't."

"When I was about sixteen he told me it was just as easy to fall in love with a rich girl as a poor girl."

"Oh I don't mind that," she said. "I like being rich and I don't mind being loved. What a shrewd man your father must have been."

"He should've been a preacher."

"You mean he was religious?"

"No, not at all. He was just good at preaching a good game. Some guy fast-talked him for all his money with a scheme about a machine called Super Scoop that would give you scoops of ice cream like you were getting Cokes at a Coke machine."

"No kidding," and she buried her head in the pillow, laughing.

"Sure. Super Scoops. He didn't want me to believe anybody because he believed everybody. He believed in everything."

"My father," she said, "only believed in himself."

"What was his problem?"

"Since when was believing in yourself a problem?"

"You just said it like he didn't believe in anybody else."

"I don't know who else he believed in. God and distilled water."

"What?"

"Distilled water. He went all over the world and wherever there was bad sewage he got big business selling distilled water. Then it all got so big and so successful there was nothing to do but retire."

She sat up in bed, a silk bedshirt falling away from her shoulders. Her breasts were small and the nipples pink. She cradled his head, caressing his throat. "He became a gardener, planting in the yard and even buying a small lot of vacant land close by so he could build a rock garden, but after that Portuguese boy was drowned in a sink, remember how it was such a big story in all the papers, killed by that lunkhead who'd sexually assaulted the boy, my father discovered the death penalty. He was determined to bring back the death penalty and he came alive like he'd never been before."

She got out of bed, collecting her garter belt and underwear, and then she said, "He became such a big public speaker. It was his whole concern and he sat for hours reading, and rolling a ball-bearing between his fingers." She had a dresser drawer packed with his collection and she spread old yellowing photographs, engravings, and accounts of condemned men on the bedsheets before him. "They're up in the eaves, too," she said. "Boxes and boxes, and rare old books. Maybe you'd like to see them, but it's so hot and narrow up there, you'll get a cramp in your back."

She sat quietly for a moment, touching her thigh, and then she crossed her legs and stroked her instep. "Bad arches. I've always had bad arches. He used to say, 'You should wear support shoes.' It got so he watched everything like a kind of cop in the months before he died. He accepted all invitations and sometimes paid his own expenses."

There was a jar of very expensive cream on the night table. She was sitting on the end of the bed, hunched over, and he took the cream and began to rub it into her back, kneading the muscles that were surprisingly hard, even knotted, and then, for a moment, her whole body seemed to relax and she let out a deep sigh, not so much of relief but aloneness, and he lifted her long hair and kissed the nape of her neck. She shivered and drew rigid again. "It gave my father pleasure," she said, "that's exactly the way he put it, it gave him pleasure arriving in an unknown town and having his hand pressed by eager men and women, the hushed attention when he spoke about the way we could kill a man, and then there was the applause and appreciation from the local police and his hotel room where he said he showered and went to bed. He kept all the photographs from those trips, there in the album I showed you, cut into ovals like rows of eggs, smiling in all of them, serene. 'Not the look of a condemned man,' he told me the week before he just dropped dead in the street."

He was sitting cross-legged and holding her from behind. "You know what's weird around here," he said. "The place is full of vases. Vases everywhere and there's never any flowers."

"My mother told me never to sleep in a room with flowers. They steal the air."

"So why not when you're awake?"

"Stealing's stealing, day or night."

"You know what else I couldn't figure, looking at all those albums?" he said.

"No."

"There's no pictures of your mother. There's only that photograph hanging in the sewing room."

The sepia portrait had been trimmed into a triangle

and framed in rococo gilt. Between the frame and the wall there were old palm fronds curling over the face of a woman with high cheekbones and wide eyes and a shining forehead.

"No, Mother wasn't a Catholic," she said. "But she always went to Mass every year on Palm Sunday. She never said why but she always laughed quietly when she went out the door and said every donkey has its day."

2

As they walked south late one night, Helen said, "Were you born around here, I mean were you born in a house?"

"Sure. I still live there."

"You're kidding. Nobody I know but me lives where they were born."

They went along shaded streets, the houses dark and the windows long and lean. Bicycles were chained to verandah railings. A police car passed and came around the block again, slowing down. "The trouble with the police is they think everyone is a criminal," she said. "They're corrupted like that. Imagine having to live with a man looking for the criminal in you." She suddenly called out to the cop, "Anything I can do to help you officer?"

"That was wonderful," Arthur said as the police car moved away.

"It was not. We should be left alone. We should all be left alone and not bothered."

"I meant you were wonderful."

She took his arm. They had to step off the sidewalk twice to avoid lawn sprinklers left on all night. "It's against the law, you know," she said. "Leaving the water on all night, but there are laws that just don't apply to some people and nobody knows it better than that cop. Nobody's more class-conscious than cops. Ever notice that?" They crossed an old footbridge over a ravine. "No," he said, "but this is it."

"What is? The ravine?"

"No. The street along the other side. I grew up by the ravine. It runs right through the centre of the city."

She stood looking along the deep length of darkness. "It's like a scar," she said.

"It's a secret place."

"I love secret places," she said. "I love it when people take me to their secret places."

There was a heavy, chilling mist and the few bridge lamps were dull and shimmering. He held her close. "This was a lousy little two-storey town when I grew up down here," he said. "Everything was two storeys, tiny ambitions." They heard foghorns down at the lake. She brushed her lips lightly against his hand. "But then I found out there were people down there in the ravine and some were on the run, fugitives from their families or from the law, and winos. You could find a drunk on the side of the hill any morning and these drifters fascinated me, living under the old iron bridge in their own little cardboard and plywood shelters. Even in the winter they were there and it's like they were drifting angels loose in the ravine, living under a big iron rainbow, and I always wondered what it must be like living under any kind of rainbow."

The front lights were on in his house. "It's still a fine sturdy place," he said, showing her the sitting room. "Of course, the rooms are narrow in these old homes. I just seem to live a narrow life," he said, laughing.

"Do you always leave the lights on?" she said.

"Yeah."

"All night?"

"Yeah. My father used to do it."

"Why?"

"Leave a light on for your mother, he used to say."

"Where was your mother?"

"She left him a note one night and took off."

"Just like that?"

"Yeah. She told him life was like a hat shop. So he said leave a light on in the shop, maybe she'll miss her old hat."

They were sitting at the back of the house in a glass-enclosed porch crowded with plants and vines and creepers, and the room was lit by a ribbon of neon light around the window ledge.

"It's strange in here," she said.

"I find it real calm," he said. There was a little white wicker chair in the corner and she sat in it surrounded by leaves and ferns. He was in an old leather easy chair.

"You sit in here watching the plants?" she asked.

"They probably watch me."

"You know, sometimes I feel my father's watching me."

"Out in the bushes."

"What bushes?"

"It's just a family joke."

"So tell me."

"Well, it's not really a joke. I mean, my father and I once got lost up north in the bush country and we sat up all night in the dark listening to the goddamnedest noises that put the fear of hell in us, and that's where he said the dead were after that, out in the bushes, or in the bush leagues."

"What in the world are the bush leagues?"

She was sitting curled up in the dark corner, arms around her knees, feeling a damp weight on her thighs. The closeness in the air frightened her. She wanted to be comforted.

"The bush leagues," he said, settling into his easy chair. "That's baseball. When you're not good enough for the big leagues you play in the bush leagues."

"Did you play in the bush leagues?"

"No. No, but my father was a sandlot third base coach, the local leagues. He was wonderful, the way he got so dressed up, his team had these kind of cobalt blue uniforms with yellow stripes down the legs and WORLD MEDIA BROKERS in yellow letters on the back, and he used to scream at the umpires."

"He sounds like someone my father would have hated."

"I don't know. Maybe. For him it was all wonderful play-acting. Sometimes he got confused on the field." He closed his eyes and she felt as if she were slowly sinking away from him into the dark earth smell of leaves and ferns. "You see, he'd wave his arms like a windmill, waving a runner home, and when the runner got called out by a country mile so everybody saw he'd made a mistake, he'd scream and yell and finally the umpire would pump his fist, yelling, *You're outa here, you're outa the game.* He'd laugh, patting his hands together like a pleased boy. That was the beautiful thing, see. To him it was all a game, it had nothing to do with life. That's what he used to say: Life's real kid, and playing baseball is playing for time. You get thrown outa life and what you are is dead."

"And your mother never came home," she asked, her voice almost a hush.

"Nope. That was real. About a year after he died I got a telegram saying she was dead, too."

"But you still keep the lights on."

"Well, you can't turn your back on the dead," he said, laughing again. "They may be out there lost in the bushes."

He stretched his legs. They sat in silence for a long time. Then she said, "I think I feel ashamed."

"Ashamed of what?" he said, reaching out to her shadow in the corner, but she was farther away than he thought.

"Nothing. I just feel this need."

He rested his elbows on his knees, his hands hanging together, staring into the ebony windows. There were always raccoons outside in the alley at night. They came up from the ravine, rummaging for food. She said fiercely, "I want to make love."

"What?"

"I need to make love.'

She stood up and stepped out of her skirt, and then her panties, and still wearing knee-high black boots, stockings, and a garter belt, she lay down, her head in the shadows, knees up and spread.

"Here?" he asked.

"Here," she said, "and hurry."

He was in his stocking feet. He couldn't grip the tiled floor. Her head was back under the chair and she was holding on to the wicker legs. "It'd be better with you on your hands and knees," he said. She got up and crouched over so that he held her shoulders, half squatted over her haunches, and he made love to her until she shuddered in small spasms and let out a keening wail. When she sank down he lay on her back filled with the perfume in her hair. He hadn't come. She said, "You didn't come, did you?" and he said, "No." She sighed and said, "That was unfair, making me cry out like that."

3

The next day, she went to Palm Springs. She sent a single rose with a note to the bookstore. He sat alone in the house at night, waiting for the phone to ring. He knew she would be all right. He just wanted the phone to ring, but she did not call. There was a lot of rain and dampness seeped into his bones. It was hard to sleep. Two weeks passed. Then she called late one night and said she was home and that she had been drinking. "No, it's not the rain," she said. "I don't care about the rain." A week later, at about two in the morning, she called and said, "If you come over, I'll take you to one of my secret places."

The streets were empty. "It's funny," she said, "the whole time I've been away I was thinking about my mother. I should've known her but I didn't know her."

"Me neither."

"But yours ran away. Mine stayed put and never seemed to be anywhere. We used to sit in her bedroom and hardly talk. She always wore nylons with seams and she'd run her hands along the seams, over and over, trying to get them straight. But they were always wobbly. And then she began going to bed early, you know, eleven, ten, then right after supper, closing the day down earlier and earlier until she never got out of bed and father took her her meals, more courtly the more he was out of her life. She seemed content, except she always said: Watch out, watch out."

"For what?"

"I don't know. She was so firm about it, indifferent to everything else except watching out. Nothing ever happened to her and nothing's happened to me, or maybe it has, but my always watching for something big to come along, well, somehow everything has seemed so small."

She drew close to him in the night air, and in a little while they went into an all-night restaurant. "This is it," she said. There were booths at the back and a horseshoe counter with full-length mirrors alongside the take-out stall. They sat at the counter in swivel chairs.

"You know," she said, "I came in here one night and there was an old man in a homburg hat sitting here." They ordered Golden Crispy Waffles from the big glossy menu. "I mean, he had a cribbage board and cards and we played for an hour, and the next night he was back but I didn't want to play again. I could see he was counting on it, but he'd forgotten to wear his hat and he was bald and I distrust men with shiny heads."

A boyish but broad-shouldered cop had walked along the mirrors to the take-out stall. He asked for a double-double coffee. "There's a sweet tooth," she said. "A sweet-tooth cop."

A man who had a lopsided gait had come in behind the cop. He hurried to an empty chair and pocketed the dollar bill that had been left behind as a tip. Then he sat down and the waitress bawled at him, "Hey, I hustle too hard for my tips, I hustle and I don't care if you're a retard or not."

"How do you like that?" Arthur asked her.

"Like what?"

"A little case of theft."

"They'll work it out," she said. "Leave them alone and they'll work it out."

The man sat staring into an empty coffee cup. There was a lipstick mark on the rim of the cup and he touched it. Then he picked up a crust of cold toast and ate it. "I don't care," the waitress said, walking over to the cop, who came back, lumbering slowly, looking a little flushed. The waitress said, "It's my tip." The cop sat down, speaking quietly to the man, saying, "It's her tip, you see. It's hers. You can understand that. You have to give it back." The man shook his head stubbornly and drew little empty egg shapes on the counter-top. The cop moved the knife and fork away.

"That's really strange," Helen said. "That's what my father used to do at every meal."

"What?"

"We had to take the knives off the table until after he said grace."

"Where the hell did he get that idea?"

"I don't know. But it sure gave a funny feel to eating when we picked up our knives."

"Come on," the cop said, "be a good guy. You've got to give it back." The man fumbled and took the dollar out of his shirt pocket. He gave it to the cop who handed it to the waitress who came over to Helen and said, "I'm sorry, but it's mine, see, because I gotta hustle."

The cop stood up and said quietly, "Come along now. It's probably best if you go home." He caught sight of himself in the mirror and flushed, as if embarrassed at how big he looked, and he frowned and said, touching the man on the shoulder, "Come on now. It's all for the best." The man stood up and they walked to the door. The cop held the door open for him. The waitress said, "I don't trust cops."

"I don't trust cops either," Helen said.

"But the cop," Arthur said, "handled it beautifully."

"I don't like cops," Helen said firmly. "I don't like cops."

"Well, maybe you're right, but the cop worked it out."

"Don't patronize me."

"We better go," he said.

"Yeah, okay," she said, rolling her napkin into a little ball. She dropped it into her empty coffee cup. He left the waitress a good tip.

"Well," she said at the door, "how do you like our first disagreement."

"It happens to the best of us," he said.

"And the worst," she said, laughing. "I'll make love to you tonight, okay?"

"We'll see," he said and put his arm firmly around her shoulders as they hailed a taxi. At home, he took off his shirt. "No, no," she said. "I want to be good to you. You can't say no to a girl who wants to be good." He was disappointed. He wanted to soothe her. "You want me up against the wall?" he said, laughing and stepping out of his shoes.

"It's nice, isn't it?"

"Yeah, except this time I want to watch."

"Whatever you want," she said and knelt down.

"How come you want to be so good to me?"

"Everything good comes to an end," she said, smiling, and held him firmly by the thighs.

He could only see her hair over her hunched shoulders and the soles of her feet, and his own unhappy look in the mirrored light.

Two days later, she called and said she had found a superb pheasant pâté. He decided to bring her a single rose. "Well," she said, taking the long thin box, "where will I put that?" She put it into the umbrella stand and took him into the library and showed him the photograph he had given her. It was on a side table, scissored and fitted into an oval upright silver frame. He was smiling in the photograph and looked very handsome.

"Don't you think it's a beautiful frame?" she said. "I got it last time in Palm Springs." She cut two little pieces of pâté and put them on delicate china plates. She was wearing a black dress buttoned to the throat, with puffed sleeves, and a handkerchief at her wrist, under the sleeve.

"Don't you like the frame?"

"Yes, of course. It's very fine. Not the look of a condemned man, either," he said, smiling. She gave him his plate of pâté and went to a carved oak cabinet.

"I think we should have a little something from my father's stock, Denis Mounié. My father told me it's the cognac of the diplomatic corps."

"To your health," he said. "We've never toasted you, and today you look very beautiful."

"Do you know," she said, "with all the things we've talked about, we've never talked about politics. Everybody talks about politics."

"That's right," he said. "And it's only fair."

"What is?" she asked gaily.

"That we should talk about politics."

They discussed the news in the papers, whether the Mayor now looked better after a small operation to correct an overbite and whether there should be a citizens' police review board, and then they walked to the vestibule. The rose was in its box, upright in the umbrella stand. She stood beside him at the open door, holding his hand. He kissed her lightly on the cheek. "Leave a little light in the window," he said. She laughed and they said goodbye.

He saw her again a month later out at the airport when he was coming in from a New York book fair. He would have called out to her but she was moving too quickly, and with all her composure, to catch a plane. It was the last time he saw her. But he had occasion to drive by her house one night. The house was in darkness. In spite of himself he stopped, waiting to see a light come on. Over the months, he often went out of his way to pass the big house, and one night the lawn sprinkler was on, but the house remained dark.

A Drawn Blind

OLDHAM AMIS LIVED IN A YELLOW BRICK HOUSE WITH a peaked slate roof. There was an old limestone hitching post half-hidden in the dogwood bushes down along the driveway. Oldham sometimes sat there on a varnished folding chair from his father's sailing sloop. His father had made a small fortune in ball bearings and had spent his money on sailing boats and stone animals carved by a friend in the mortuary business. He'd decorated the front lawn with stone puppies, fawns, and lion cubs and inside the house there were brass wind-lamps on the walls and cane deck furniture in the drawing room. There was a big polished brass bell hanging over the bathtub in the bathroom.

His mother had always kept to herself, cradling two Siamese cats who sometimes in the early morning went out of the house and killed sparrows and left them on the front stoop. She kept scented handkerchiefs in her sleeve and used them to touch her temples while she read romances by Mazo de la Roche, and when her husband drowned in a squall on Lake Scugog, she went out to the garage and got a tire iron and smashed all the stone animals on the lawn. Oldham, then nearly nineteen, came home and found her sitting on a white wicker stool in the bathroom and she was running boiling water into the open tub and the room was dense with steam and she was methodically clanging the brass bell.

Oldham, after he'd entered teacher's college, kept his mother company in the late afternoons and he tried reading aloud the gossip in the newspapers but she had become a secret drinker and her mind wandered as she sat wrapped in a blanket on the verandah, sipping gin from a bone china cup. He sat in silence as the sun went down, his long legs stretched out and crossed at the ankles, because there was little more he could say to her. She only cared about Slavs and Jews and their noisy children who were moving onto the street from the South Market.

"Don't you see," she had cried one evening, touching her temple with a little white lace handkerchief, "we're all fakes, like Mazo de la Roche. Did you know her real name was really Mazie Roche? They're overrunning us, those scum, listen to them, and we deserve it, no backbone, any of us."

Sometimes when the children were playing street hockey she'd call the police and in a little while a yellow patrol car would ease around the corner and a cop would tell the noisy kids to get off the street.

"That's all that's left to count on," she'd say, "the police."

When his mother died he was secure but he kept on teaching history at the Collegiate up on the hill because he liked talking about the mistakes generals made, how history, especially when men were at their most optimistic, was always in decline. In a small book about a courtesan who'd inexplicably committed suicide, he found the epitaph he had carved on his mother's headstone: "Tired of this eternal buttoning and unbuttoning." His father's old friend, the mortician, was offended, but he didn't care. He began to collect books of epitaphs and when he found out that the hill his school was on had been called Gallows Hill because the blue clay had been used to make the bricks for the first death house in the city, he felt a warm confirmation of his sense of how things secretly hung together, and that was the pleasure he sought in all his books, a confirmation of how he felt about life. He didn't talk to many people and didn't change his mind about many things, and even though the house was filled with all kinds of books, their clutter irritated him, they were in his way. He didn't want to reread them and yet, because they had been expensive, he couldn't bring himself to give them away or throw them out.

Then one day in a subway station he saw the ticket-taker in the glass cage reading a paperback book, and the man, rather than set the book down and mark his place, would just tear off the cover and then tear off the pages as he finished them, dropping them into a waste can, whittling the book down to nothing. This seemed so sensible to Oldham that from then on he read only paperbacks and even when he sat reading on the front lawn by the old hitching post he placed a little waste can down beside his right shoe.

Then one evening when he was listening to the opening innings of a baseball game, the evening sun filtering through the silver birch trees, the living room in a lovely rose washlight, he sat drinking brandy in his rush-bottomed ladderback chair beside the old upright radio and wrote in a neat cramped hand in a book of blank pages bound in black leather. For nearly three months he'd been keeping a journal, not what he did from day to day, but notes and small reflections, and while sitting listening to the broadcast of the ball game and Mudcat Cleever who was pitching a no-hitter, he wrote: "The deepest root desire we have is to project totally ourselves, cookie-shapes of who we are; hence, Adam's rib becomes Eve so that he can copulate with his image of himself, and the Virgin, she conceives her son out of herself; love thyself as thy neighbour. . . ."

He took off his round steel-rimmed glasses and sat with his eyes closed, half-brooding, half-listening. Then, by the seventh inning of the ball game, he was so caught up in Cleever's no-hitter that he suddenly realized he was sitting in total darkness. He wanted to share his excitement because he was on the edge of his chair, hanging on every pitch, but he found himself touched by a bit-tersweetness and surprise and a flutter of panic because he'd never seen himself as so absolutely alone, and as he stood up he remembered the first time as a boy that he'd been in his father's boat in rough water, and he'd lain down on the deck refusing to look at the waves that smashed broadside and with his eyes shut he'd repeated over and over, "Jesus Mary and Joseph," just like he'd heard his mother moaning one late evening alone in the kitchen, but on the boat his father kept calling out, "Nothing can go wrong, Oldie old kid," and nothing had gone wrong and Oldham had been ashamed but his father had said, "You got to feel fear at least once to find out what it is and once you know, then you know how to handle it," and Oldham, in the dark of his living room, alone, suddenly smiled, feeling buoyant and unafraid and at ease. He went out for a long walk, forgetting about Cleever and the baseball game.

The more he thought about it the more he liked being alone. He didn't like talking to women for too long and was glad he taught in an all-boys school. Standing by himself in a crowd, or sitting at a bar, his sense of his own aloofness gave him a feeling of security, as if he couldn't be touched, and also a sense of self-discipline. Of an evening, after he'd marked his class papers, and he was a stern marker, he'd go to the movies or a club if there was a good Dixieland band on the stand, and once a week he had supper in the Oak Room in the King Edward Hotel, usually milk-fed veal or medallions of beef in wine and mushroom sauce. Then he walked along to the Dundas Street strip-joints, watched the show, and hired one of the hookers who lined the lounge walls every night. He liked his no-nonsense approach to the whole matter and though he kept his little notes to himself in his leather-bound book, he was sure too much reflection, too much analysis of the self, was a kind of self-hatred, and he was delighted one night when he found a quote, unattributed, in a collection of epitaphs: "Nowadays not even a suicide kills himself in desperation. Before taking the step he deliberates so long and so carefully that he literally chokes with thought. It is even questionable whether he ought to be called a suicide, since it is really thought which takes his life. He does not die with deliberation, but from deliberation."

Then late one night there was a soft rain, a falling mist, and when he went out to sit on the verandah around midnight, the street lamps glowing up in the caves of leaves in the maple trees touched him with an almost sensual longing, not for anything lost in the past, because he had no particular regrets, but it was a kind of home-sickness for the future, a wondering whether in the midst of his calmness he was already into his decline, and was he going to end in a fog like his mother or suddenly disappear under water like his father.

As he sat with his arms folded across his chest, hugging himself because he felt an evening chill, he looked at the houses across the road, thinking they were like a row of crypts in the night, and he began to look up and down the street for lights in the windows, wondering what went on in all those darkened rooms, because the big old homes were now rooming houses filled with blacks and haggard whites.

He began walking late at night when the streets were empty, nearly everyone asleep except for a few random lights, and in those windows the blinds were always drawn, making the light seem secret and more mysterious. He found himself making up little scenes, imagining what was going on behind those blinds, as if he'd walked quickly by an open doorway in one of the downtown hooker hotels and seen bodies caught in a flash of light and then they were gone, no names, forgotten, and this left him with the same feeling as he had sitting down to supper in the Oak Room, where he was part of the place and yet apart. He didn't want to meet any of the people who lived in the houses any more than he would have spoken to people in those rooms in the hotels, but he liked thinking that there were transient lives being lived in the half-light of those rooms, lives as mysterious as his own, because he thought with a sudden rush of satisfaction that if anyone were to pay any particular attention to him, surely he would seem a mysterious self-enclosed man to his neighbours. Certainly motorcycle policemen going by slowly at one and two in the morning gave him a quizzical look as he sauntered along the sidewalk in his tweed jacket.

One night, he heard the low, mournful wail of a horn and as he stood listening it sounded like someone playing the Last Post, and so he went out into the street just in time to see a woman in slacks running away through the shadows toward Dupont Street. There was a light in the big front room on the second floor in the house across the street. Someone was pacing back and forth behind the drawn blind. Out on the balcony, a man stood playing a trombone, the horn angled up into the air. A short bald man dressed only in slippers and dressing gown sidled up to Oldham on the lawn and said, "Must be up there I bet."

Oldham said, "Yes, that's it," suddenly overcome with the feeling that the man up there with his arms outstretched was reaching out only to him, and that if he only had a horn himself, if only he'd known how to play, he would've stood there on his lawn and blown back at the man outlined against the dark sky, but instead he said over again, "Yes, that's it." Then a woman wearing a pink taffeta housecoat and pink pom-pom slippers joined them, saying, "Now there's a wacky son-of-a-bitch. You never know what's gonna happen in the night." The man on the balcony, who was only a shadow in the light from the half-hidden moon, was playing the same mournful notes, over and over again, so sonorous that they were chilling, but the bald man began to laugh. Oldham was offended by the laughter.

The police came in a black unmarked patrol car and Oldham stood beside the car waiting while the officers went into the house. Then one of them appeared on the balcony and led the trombone player inside. The car window was open and Oldham could hear the dry rasping voice of the dispatcher over the radio. The woman in pom-poms who'd come up beside him said, "Lots of action tonight, someone's always screwing someone." Then the young policeman came down the walk, smiling, and Oldham said, "What's the matter?" The cop with the blond moustache said, "Nothing important, guy came home and found his wife in bed with her girlfriend. More of that going on all the time." They drove away.

Oldham found himself brooding about the police and the horn player and the woman fleeing up the street, and the next day during classes he was distracted and strangely troubled. Two or three times he stood silently nodding his head, and later that night while he was walking he said to himself, "What'd that dumb dope mean saying it was nothing important." He felt full of rage and also a sadness for that lonely horn player. A motorcycle cop ahead was riding half out of his saddle seat, methodically moving along past the row of parked cars. His motor broke the silence with its dry spluttering and Oldham saw that he had a thick stub of chalk in his hand and he was reaching out, swiping at the back wheels, leaving a white slash on the tires. He realized the cop was marking cars, that they'd all get overnight parking tags in the morning, and because the streets around were lined with cars with no place to park he said to himself, "Why, that's like shooting sitting ducks."

The next night he carried a damp cloth rolled in a ball in his hand, and he was tense as he walked along the roadway, dipping down at the back wheel of every car, wiping away the chalk marks. It took him about three-quarters of an hour to cover two blocks. He worked up a sweat. Then he quit because on the other streets he didn't know any of the houses and there were no lights in the windows. They weren't his neighbours.

One week later, he nodded laconically to a motorcy-cle cop wearing a white helmet and the cop scowled back at him and the next night he met the same cop on foot. He realized the cop was trying to catch him, and he laughed quietly, but when the cop said, "You better watch out," he stepped forward, stern and officious, as if he were dealing with a recalcitrant boy in his classroom, calling into the startled cop's face, "I beg your pardon," and the cop took a step sideways with Oldham pursuing him, saying again, even more aggressively, "I beg your pardon, I beg your pardon." Then he turned and went back home, leaving the cop alone out in the street.

As he walked up alongside his dogwood bushes, he looked back at the windows across the street, all of them dark, and he thought how gradually during the week it must have dawned on those people in the morning that there'd been no tickets on their windshields, and what pleased him was that they would have no idea why the tickets had suddenly stopped and they wouldn't know who to ask or even what had gone on. He felt so good as he went into the house that he went upstairs and pulled down the blind in the bathroom window and took off his clothes and got into the tub and took a hot bath. As he stretched out in the soothing water he smiled, knowing that if anyone were standing out in the back in the dark looking up at the light behind his drawn blind they'd have no idea of how secretly satisfied he was.

Prowlers

SLAVERNE TUTTLE'S MOTHER WANTED A GIRL. SHE loved the name Laverne, but when he was born a boy she settled for Slaverne and kept him in long curls until he was seven, when children on the street clipped his hair in the rose garden with a pair of pruning shears. His mother cried, but he took the clipping calmly. His father died during the war, parachuting behind enemy lines. He had only a faint recollection of a small man with steel-rimmed glasses, but his mother was tall with a blade nose, a pastor's daughter who became morose sitting alone listening for her husband's step. "He had a slight limp," she said. Slaverne grew up feeling sorry for his mother, and one night he came home and found her drunk before the fire, dressed in her white wedding gown, and he said, "I am the man in your life, Mother." She cracked him across the face and wept as he tried to hold her, blood from his nose staining her dress.

It was only after she died that he began wearing her clothes. During the day, he worked as a court clerk and he enjoyed the work, sitting at his own oval table, his long

fingers moving like spiders silently over the keys. Sometimes, a judge asked him to read the evidence aloud. He
always smoothed his closely cropped hair, quietly clipping
his words. One judge told him testily that his thin
monotone made all testimony sound the same. "The
world is full of impassioned pleas," the judge said. "And
none of us are the same. Never forget that." The judge had
gathered his black robes and swept into his chambers,
nodding at tight-lipped attorneys wearing white bibs. "It's
the due process," Slaverne told his friend Charlie, who
was a long-distance bus driver. "You look at these people
and you know it's all a question of who's in their high-heel
sneakers. The cops strut around in crash helmets like
space thugs, the hookers play pouting virgins. It's all a
laugh. No matter how you look at it, life is a costume
contest, Charlie, and don't you forget it. We're not
weird."

He had met Charlie, who had a long thin nose and
hooded eyes that were languid and sensual after only a
touch of eye shadow, at an indoor shooting range. They
shared a love of high-powered pistols and the oiled sheen
of the barrel as they stood side by side, insulated from the
echoing shots by big padded ear-cups. Charlie was also
good at pruning roses.

He often stayed with Slaverne after coming in off the
road. He had his own closet in the small frame house set
back from the street in a downtown cul-de-sac. The
kitchen and music room looked out on the garden of roses,
honeysuckle and dogwood. Slaverne liked the garden
because it seemed secluded. "Those are the enemy lines
out there," he'd told Charlie, but sometimes drifters came

down the cul-de-sac and fell into step behind him late at night. He often thought he was being shadowed, and one night he broke into a run, furious at people who wouldn't leave him alone. When he got to the house and looked back down the dimly lit road, there was no one there. Disconcerted, he doubled back, watching for movement in the bushes. He knew there were always prowlers watching and peeping in the bushes behind the house, because on hot summer evenings with the windows open he had heard a twig snap or a muffled cough.

Charlie was easygoing and had a sensuous slow walk. He got out of his uniform as soon as he was in the house and put on lace underclothes and a little jewelry. He usually cooked supper wearing a brassiere, a half-slip, and Lucite heels. He knew his legs were long and lovely. He seldom closed the kitchen curtains and Slaverne, sensing someone out in the dark, would see a shadow pass. He spoke sharply to Charlie about walking around half-naked as if they were alone and had all the freedom in the world. "We don't, you know," he said sourly. "Everybody's a criminal these days."

Charlie always said he was sorry and closed the curtains and the drapes in the music room and curled up beside Slaverne on the small sofa. Slaverne kissed his closed eyes, but they were becoming more curt with each other, and Slaverne thought Charlie was turning into a showoff, wearing a leather suit to a party one night with a parachute pack strapped to his back. There were several small bottles of champagne in the pack, and Charlie had been the centre of attention even though he was a small man, smaller than Slaverne, who was lithe and lean. "Look at me," Slaverne had said testily, "here I am in my late thirties and I still look like a track star." He felt lethargic about their affair and he blamed Charlie.

"Maybe the trouble is you don't love me any more," Charlie said one night.

"Don't be silly," Slaverne said. "You're beautiful."

"Who's silly. I take off my clothes and you look like you're looking through me."

"What can I say?"

"Say something."

"Maybe we've known each other too long, maybe clothes make the man," he said, crossing his legs.

"Since when is two years too long?"

"I mean maybe we're used to each other, that's all. People get used to each other."

"Yeah, well not me. I never know what you're doing."

"Maybe that's the trouble," he said. "I don't get any surprises any more."

"So what am I supposed to do, hop-dance with a dildo?"

"Look, I'm just telling you I feel boxed in. Maybe we need to take another look at each other. What do I know about why I feel this way?"

"If you don't know, who does?"

Slaverne heard a noise outside. He parted the drapes and looked into the darkness, listening for footsteps. On another evening, he had caught a glimpse of a man limping up the garden slope and he had called the police and waited nearly two hours for them to come, but they never did and he went to bed with Charlie feeling angry and betrayed because the police hadn't taken the invasion of his privacy seriously.

He knew there were prowlers out in the garden every night, sitting on their haunches in the shrubbery. There were several small apartment buildings close by, and the peepers were looking for women who had forgotten themselves and left a little opening of light into their bedrooms as they undressed. Slaverne and Charlie now made love in the dark.

Then one day Charlie received an unsigned note in the mailbox from a man who said he had seen her though the kitchen window, "because there you were in your underclothes and didn't seem to care, so I'd like to say hello, it'd be terrific if you'd call the enclosed number at three in the afternoon on Tuesday. It's a pay phone and I'll be there and I'll know it's you and you don't have to feel self-conscious because we won't be able to see each other."

Charlie promised to keep the curtains closed but Slaverne sat around feeling sour because someone had stood undisturbed in the dark watching Charlie. "I don't count. I mean if he's seen you, he's seen me, he knows I'm here, I'm the man of the house, but you're just supposed to phone some phone booth like I don't exist." He threw open the living room drapes and stood scowling into the darkness.

A few nights later, Slaverne heard slow steps through the long grass. It was late at night and he and Charlie were dressing for a pre-Lenten ball. Some of the most dashing dowagers were expected and Slaverne had said excitedly, "We're going to prowl in the owl hours tonight." He was wearing a silver lamé sheath, a beautiful brunette wig, his mother's pearls, and red patent-leather shoes. Charlie, always a little late, was still in lace under-things. Slaverne parted the drapes and there by the kitchen window, pale, almost putty-faced, was a young man wearing little round glasses. "That's it," Slaverne said, "that does it," as he watched the young man go up the slope of the back garden followed by a little black-and-white terrier.

Charlie, who had washed his hair in the kitchen sink and had a towel wrapped around his head, told Slaverne to phone the police. Slaverne cursed and went to his bed-room closet and took down the pistol case. He came back into the kitchen, saying, "Don't worry, it isn't loaded." Charlie laughed. "You should see yourself," he said. Slaverne stood handling the gun for weight, as if its balance were suddenly important, and he said, "I'm going to scare the living Jesus out of that punk, that's all." He went along the hall at a half-trot in his high heels, hoping no one would see him, hunching down as he went out the back door into the cover of the bushes.

He angled up the side of the slope and held close to a big sugar-maple tree, his heels sinking into the soft earth, certain he couldn't be seen. He held the pistol along the length of his leg and heard steps and the snuffling of a dog in the underbrush, and then there was a shadow on the other side of the tree. He stepped out and said in his thin, clipped voice, "Hold it right there you son-of-a-bitch." He was surprised when the young man, backing away from the gun, said, "You're crazy." Slaverne, peering at him in the shadow-light, said, "I am not." He was trying to sound reasonable, but he was suddenly afraid the boy might attack him. The unloaded gun was useless and he felt confused, but then the boy bent down and cradled the small dog. "You're crazy, lady," he said, "and I'm going home."

"You're not going anywhere," Slaverne said, his voice rising.

"Oh yeah," and the boy turned. He was clutching the dog to his chest. The frightened dog's little legs were pedalling in the air. "You bet I am so going home," he said. "There's no way no crazy dame is gonna shoot me. You're crazy but not that crazy." Hesitant, and then suddenly hurrying, he started walking around the house toward the street. Slaverne, trying not to hook his heels in any loose roots, got into step behind him, saying, "Maybe so, but get out of line and I'll knock your head off with this thing." The boy kept going. As they passed the music room window, Charlie, wearing a brassiere and half-slip, almost luminous in the box of amber window-light, appeared. He had brushed out his long black wig and he looked more beautiful than Slaverne had ever seen him, so beautiful that he wanted to stop and stand there in the darkness and stare. He had never seen Charlie in that light before, but the boy was leading him along the walk to the street and Slaverne was suddenly furious at Charlie for always parading in the windows and he screamed, "For God's sake, close the curtains. That's the end. Close the curtains and get out." He tried to cradle the pistol casually in the crook of his arm.

"Where we going, lady?" the boy asked when they got to the road.

"What do you mean where are we going?" Slaverne said.

"Where we going?" the boy said, darting across the road.

"The cops," Slaverne blurted out, hurrying after him.

"I don't see no cops."

"The cops are all over the place," Slaverne said, because every night policemen in yellow patrol cars came down the dead-end street and put parking tickets on all the cars. "Yeah, the cops," Slaverne said as he looked up and down the empty road.

The boy strode between some low bushes in a small park, going toward the busy downtown streets. Slaverne saw that city gardeners had cut back the bushes. He circled around so that he wouldn't catch his dress. It was Saturday night and he knew everyone would be crowding into restaurants after the late shows.

"Why the hell were you peeping anyway?" Slaverne called out. He was several strides behind the boy.

"I'm not a peeper."

"Sure, you're just walking your dog."

"That's right," the boy said, "and there's no law against that, but I'll bet there's a law against you poking that gun at me."

"You were looking in my window," Slaverne said, shifting the pistol to his other hand, "and anyway, you want to look at bare boobs, the bars are full of naked bimbos."

"I don't drink," the boy said, "and besides, I'm underage. I'd be breaking the law."

"Are you crazy," Slaverne cried. "You're a peeper, I caught you peeping."

"No I'm not," the boy said.

"Well maybe," he said, suddenly wondering what he would do if the boy could prove to the police that he was not a Peeping Tom, and he said, "What's your name?"

"You are crazy," the boy said over his shoulder. "You think I'd tell you my name?"

"Why not?"

"You're weird," the boy said, and then he stopped and turned around, circling around Slaverne in the dark, staring at him intently, and suddenly he bawled out, "Jesus Christ, you're a fucking guy. You're a fucking guy in a fucking dress."

"You're goddamn right and I'm just liable to do anything, you lousy little punk," Slaverne cried as the boy hurried off toward Bleeker Street and all the Chinese restaurants. As they came out under the rippling neon signs, Slaverne heard his name called out and he looked back and saw Charlie hurrying up the hill in his bare feet, holding his long skirt with one hand and his high-heel shoes with the other. Slaverne and the boy, shoulder to shoulder for a moment by the curb, stared into the luminous red and yellow lettering and the flashing head-lights. Slaverne suddenly ducked his head, as if they were all on him, and he let the pistol dangle along his leg. The boy, surrounded by all the light and suddenly laughing, stepped into the traffic and Slaverne was nearly hit by a taxi as he went after him and leapt sideways, carrying the pistol high in the air.

People stared. Slaverne ran across the street after the

boy, but before he could threaten him, the boy turned. He had taken off his steel-rimmed glasses and he had muddy little eyes and, laughing, he said, "You goddamn stupid queen. Let's go to the goddamn police station, eh! You think the cops'll let a crazy freak like you go around the streets with a gun?" Charlie, having stepped into his high heels on the other side of the street, looking stylish and elegant, was parading through the cars, letting a lace handkerchief dangle in the air, stopping traffic. Putting down his little dog, the boy strode off toward the police station.

Slaverne kept stride for a few moments with the boy but men and women seeing the gun suddenly stepped aside, glaring, and someone cried out, "What are you, lady, crazy?" He yelled, "Mind your own fucking business." Then the boy turned and screamed, "He's a goddamn freak, he's a goddamn guy in a dress." An elderly couple recoiled just as Charlie, wearing a black velvet dress with a scoop neck, took Slaverne's arm. The boy was now far ahead, looking over his shoulder, and then he ran off into the crowd, the terrier scampering after him. Slaverne was suddenly frightened and he cursed, seeing himself trailing his dress along a dusty courtroom floor, a white-bibbed attorney pleading, "None of us are the same, Your Honour." He lifted his slit skirt and jammed the pistol into his garter belt along the inside of his thigh. Charlie was giggling. Across the road, Chinese waiters all wearing burgundy serving-jackets were lined up along the curb, waving and laughing.

"It's all your damn fault," Slaverne screamed at Charlie.

"My fault. You charge out of the house like a crazy man with a gun and it's my fault."

"I told you to get out. Get out of my life. You've humiliated me."

He grabbed Charlie by the shoulders and spun him into the darkened doorway of a grocery store. There were shining steel hooks in the window and two pressed ducks on white tiles under the hooks. "You tart," Charlie yelled. "You goddamn pretentious tart."

Slaverne, with all the neon light catching his silver lamé dress, cracked Charlie across the face and Charlie screamed, letting go a looping left. He missed and they wrestled to the curb and Charlie, his nose bleeding, wobbled on his high heels and turned an ankle. Slaverne knocked him down. The waiters on the other side of the street yelled. One called out, "Yankee imperialists go home."

A sloppily dressed man, a drifter, sauntered drunkenly along and stood over Charlie who lay tangled up in his long velvet dress. The drifter said, "Aw, come on." Slaverne punched him in the face and the drunk collapsed and began to cry. Slaverne strutted into the street, crossing toward the waiters, smoothing his dress and hair, trembling. There was a little blood on his dress. He suddenly threw his shoulders back. He knew that his legs looked good.

"Well, it's a man's world," he called to the waiters, wheezing for air, his voice deep. There was giggling laughter. He adjusted his wig as a car came along and spun on his heel, hiking up his skirt, hitching a ride with his thumb out in the air. The driver hunched forward over his wheel and stopped; he reached across the front seat and opened the door, smiling smugly at the waiters. Slaverne saw Charlie crawling out of the doorway, his velvet dress torn at the shoulder strap. Slaverne slipped into the front seat and with his face framed in the window he blew the waiters a Hedy Lamarr kiss. As the car sped off, the waiters broke into applause.

And So to Bed

ALL MY FRIENDS CALL ME BOOKER, NOT BECAUSE I make book on the ponies or because I take after Booker T. Washington White who was a slope-headed blues singer, but because I'm into books, not like a book worm, but a dipper. I am a dipper. I walk up the beach of my mind looking for ash trays in their wild state and POW. That's what I want, a POW on the page. So I buy two or three books a week and put my boots up and read them in the morning beside the window in my waterfront flat which I get cheap because it's down by the warehouses where I've got a good view of the bay. Sometimes I go down to the docks and take a ferry to the island, just reading in the sun like there's no tomorrow, which I know there is because really I'm optimistic. I always hope for the best, and I do believe you always make your own luck. So I sit on the upper deck, dipping into a page when I've got an empty moment free from thinking. It's like picking a pocket, just like old Matthew Arnold, who was a kind of pickpocket, said it. The special moments when you see something real clear are everything, they're the touch-stones. Some people touch wood, I touch stone.

But make no mistake, old Booker is not touched in the head. Booker breaks loose in the evening. I mean, I try never to read at night, 'cause night reading is like the night air, you can catch your death of cold. So I prance and play, *I got the sun in the morning and the daughter at night.* That's my song, and these days the song's getting sung at this small tiny nightclub that's got those plush velvet booths and an oval stage. Ovals always remind me of eggs. Big beginnings. And the new club singer, she's got this great billboard name, Empress Angel Eyes, and a long loping walk with great legs like she just came in off the *veldt* out of some movie starring Meryl Streep doing another accent instead of acting. I like that. Anyway, the Empress showed me the other night an old picture of herself from years back playing the mouth harp and wearing little granny glasses. "You want to get anywhere," she says, "you got to look like whatever's going on. Granny glasses one day, décolletage the next. And I tell you," she said, sipping a double scotch-on-the-rocks, "as singers go, Piaf had it lucky. Everybody wants to break your heart like Piaf except she breaks your heart better."

"Great God almighty," I said, "you're bang-on, you're right. Piaf's always been the touchstone."

"The what?"

"Once you've heard Piaf sing you've heard the song," I said, and she says, "Yeah, I guess that's true. . . but you haven't heard me," and I said, "No, no, I haven't heard you," except I had, standing at the back of the nightclub the night before and she was no Piaf, nor was meant to be, but she could break my heart anytime, so — "That's a goddam great insight," I said, and I meant it: "You're terrific, you know that?"

"No," she said, flat-out and dead-pan like the thought had never crossed her mind. Which made me say, "Baby, you've got happenings going on, and happenings, in case you don't know, are when the light shines in your eyes full of surprise." She was wearing silver cowboy boots. She smoked Lucky Strikes. Her corn-yellow hair had this great luminous glow in the lights from the stage. "You know what?" she said. "When I was sixteen I slept with Janis Joplin the week before she died. I was just a kid of course, looking for a little life. Action, you know." She threw her head back and laughed. She had those great full breasts and right away I wanted to make love to her.

"I got to be careful," she said, smiling.

"About what?"

"I been hurt a lot, man, so don't hurt me."

"You know," I said, "little moments like this are wonderful." I kissed her on the cheek, just this delicate little brush like she's got no heavy duty trouble coming down on her from me. "Sometimes," I said, settling back so she could see she should relax herself, "I sit watching the water out my window, I live down by the waterfront, all the little whitecaps are like special little moments, little moments like this."

Right then, Eddie Burke, the owner of the club, who's heavyset with these hooded eyes and a real sour temper like he sucks lemons to start the day and swallows the seeds, he sat down and said, "Getting to know my little Empress, eh?" He laughed, because actually we get along okay. I know he likes to gaff with the goof butts behind the timpany, and like all potheads he's possessive, which is why — when they get arrested — it's for possession. I like that. So he folded his hand over hers. "Before you," he said to her, "I had me an old black scat singer in here. I fired him in three nights. I found him fooling with one of the waitresses, man, and it wasn't because the old fucker was black. It was because he was old. I couldn't stand the idea of that old buzzard nosing around one of my tender tits." I laughed pretty much because Eddie expected me to laugh, but I took the little warning to heart because I was meant to and Angel Eyes stood up and went to change for her show and I said, "The world is too much with us, man." So me and Eddie locked hands across the table. After all, we'd been good casual friends for a few years, and good casual friends are hard to find. "I got a gut feeling for women," Eddie said, "and I'd really like to bag that woman, but mostly I like young girls. I shag young girls because I got a gut feeling for life." I saw that Eddie was a little looped, so I said:

> Nothing can be sole or whole
> That has not first been rent.

Eddie held my hand. He held it hard, with real feeling. "You're right," he said. "Don't nothing work if you don't pay the rent."

We usually talked a lot upstairs in a small room where he had all these old Rock-Revolution posters on the walls and Art Deco mirrors and all kinds of love shit stuff from the sixties like flowers and Mao doing his famous imitation of a dead moon with eyes and this fantastic wrought-iron rack of scented votive candles in the shape of a heart. Eddie had stolen it from an old empty country church.

"I don't pray but I'm all heart," he always said, sitting there beaming at the lit candles. There were two wide-assed easy chairs, some floor pillows, and a small brown rug that the first night she was up there Angel Eyes said looked like a trap door, and she sat cross-legged on the rug and said, "One day, you watch, I'm gonna drop outa sight," and I said, "Angel, you are outa sight."

So we sat drinking whisky, with me talking to her about old black blues singers I had met in bars once or twice, like Mississippi John Hurt and Otis Spann, both of them dead, and she made me remember all my little stories about those guys and what I had read about them, and I told her these stories like their deaths had really touched me, which they had, they must have, because pretty soon I was sitting there as silent as a dog on a dead-end street humming *How long's that old train been gone,* staring blankly I guess until she said, "Don't worry, man, someday the sun's gonna shine." I looked up and said nothing, but when she hunched forward in front of me on the prayer rug, I laid my hand on her shoulder like I was the book of revelation, as cool as the breeze on Lake Louise, and I said, "Angel, you're the apple of my eye," and then I whispered:

> *God appears, and God is Light.*
> *To those poor souls who dwell in Night.*

Angel Eyes got all restless and shivery and touched my hand. "Man, God is dead," she said, as serious as serious could be. "He's dead, and you ain't heard the good news, we're free. Poems like that don't mean nothing."

"They mean the whole thing's gone to hell, Angel," I said, and I got to own up I was a little wounded because she didn't seem surprised at all that I could quote so much poetry, like the woods are full of guys quoting poetry when there aren't even any woods anymore.

"You believe that?" she says.

"Believe what?"

"Hell'n stuff like that, you believe in God'n stuff like that?"

"Angel Eyes," and I tried to be reasonable, "that's not the question."

"Oh yeah, then what's the question on my mind?"

"Angel," I said, leaning close to her, "the question is, does God believe in me?"

"Oh, wow," she said, clapping her hands. "I like that, yeah, I can dig it."

"Pow," I said, because I knew I'd got her, and suddenly she kissed me on the mouth, so sweet, so delectable, so I kept coming back night after night, figuring we'd get down to a little booty, not to say some serious sex, but she kept an aloof air, and I mean aloof, like for us to get the garden of love going we were going to have to go all the way down to Florida and check into a beachfront motel, open up the windows and wait for hurricanes to blow the seeds in from Cuba. Yet in the bar, she's carrying on every night like she's open to any man who speaks to her, always listening like she's waiting for the right word to get said to her. Which drops the lead right out of my dick, I can tell you. Because I am nothing if not words. I know that for a damn natural fact. I am a word-smith. So after all these nights of stalling I've got to wonder, I've got to wonder if this woman's got any discretion. Is there any discretion in her ignition? I like that. Then, one night, I heard Eddie whisper to her, saying he really liked the way she spoke so softly and she said, "Most women got voices that could cut glass." Eddie put his hand on the small of her back like he is the only proprietor of all the property in the world, but she took his hand away, and I liked that, her shoulders back so that her breasts, sitting there so free under her sweater, looked full, and as she walked away Eddie said to me, "That's some tender trap I got singing for me, but she's too hard to get. I think she must be a little dykey." And I watched these other men like bird dogs hovering around her every night but I held to the shadows, me and Dick Tracy, trying to draw her eye, standing aside, and sometimes our eyes did meet and I smiled like I knew all that there was to know, and one night I said, "I bet you got a dimple in the small of your back."

So early one morning, after the two a.m. show, when Angel Eyes asked me if I'd rather go upstairs to drink with Eddie or sit and talk, I decided to hang out with her in the dark bar. "I wanted to sit with you tonight," she said. "I like your voice, you know that? Deep. I go by a man's voice." So we talked about this and that, keeping it light, but my voice deep the way she liked. When I got up to go home I touched her on the cheek and said, "You're still the apple of my eye." The next night I sat down beside her and whispered aloud to her a little poem:

> *The invisible worm*
> *That flies in the night,*
> *In the howling storm,*

Has found out thy bed
Of crimson joy:
And his dark secret love
Does thy life destroy.

She said she didn't know what it meant but it sounded wonderful. Then I told her about all the little things I'd noticed around town that afternoon, my little white moments I called them, white because they were what they were until we made them into what we wanted them to be, like walking on a quiet street and seeing what I thought was a dressed up fifteen-year-old boy. "He was wearing a little suit jacket with peaked lapels and a porkpie hat, and it turned out he was a man of about seventy or so and he had this rod with a little black box on the end of it in his hand, a battery box, and under the rod, moving along on the sidewalk by remote control I guess, was this tin car the size of his shoe and I said, 'What're you doing' and he said, 'I'm walking my car,' and he kept on going. He fucking well kept on going, walking his car." She laughed quietly and touched my hand, like for the first time she really cared, and I wondered what it was about a guy walking his toy car that would make her care.

"You're nice," she said. "I figure you talk just like those books you're always reading."

"Well," I said, "I try to be nice. Touch stone."

"Touch what?"

"It's just a little joke."

"You're very nice," she said, and smiled.

"You don't know," I said, "how nice I can be. I've got shunts and bunts little girls don't know."

"Oh, I believe it," she said. She squeezed my hand and then went on stage, singing like she was singing for me:

Never's just the echo of forever,
Lonesome as a love that might have been.

I went upstairs and drank whiskey for an hour with Eddie and when I came down Angel Eyes asked if we wouldn't like to go for Chinese food. The restaurant was a regular favourite all-night place for people who were in show business. The teapots were filled with cognac or champagne. Which is what show biz is. Teapots of champagne. I like that. And there was this ventriloquist at the next table talking like Mortimer Snerd, "Snerd's Words For The Birds," — *Still water runs wet* — and everyone laughed and got drunk, and Eddie tried to tap-dance, more tap than dance, because what he really liked to do was to dance on other people's heads, and then as the dawn came, Angel Eyes said, "The Empress wants to go home." Looking at me like there's no tomorrow, she says, "You making it my way?"

"Sure," I said, so surprised and drunk I found myself shaking hands with her.

Eddie scowled and I had this uneasy feeling that our friendship had just gone the way of a rat's lunch. We were no longer going to be casual on the beach. As Angel Eyes and I stood in the street, a real chill on the air in the dawn light, I buried my face in her hair, as much to keep from falling down as anything else, and whispered:

The wan moon sets behind the white wave,
And time is setting with me, Oh.

"Oh," she said, and I nestled in her arms in the taxi, my eyes closed to keep off the glare of light.

"It's real weird that I should be a singer," she said out of nowhere, "because my father was a mute."

"A mute?"

"Yeah. I would sing to him and he would sit there smiling with his mouth open."

"Nothing?"

"Nope. Not a word. It's weird, and I never told anyone that," she whispered, "so I guess I feel real close to you. Every time you speak I have to close my knees."

"Oh yeah?"

"You got that voice."

She lived by herself in a small bachelor flat. I was tired and up to my eyeballs in booze and stood with my back to the wall as she unlocked the door. Inside, she got to undressing without a word and so I got undressed, too, saying, "Baby, this is gonna be the best. I told you we'd be the best and this is going to be it. Believe you me." When we were naked I looked at her and said, "Beautiful, you got great breasts." I felt like I'd been punched to kingdom come by drink and didn't know where my dick was. "Hamlet," I said, "are you going to eat your peach or pack it in?" But I was limp all over. She touched my throat, which made me jump, and then she lay down on the white sheets. When I touched the inside of her thigh she began to sigh, this slow humming, like amazing grace. *Ummh*, she goes, *ummh*, and my blood was all in my head, in my eyes, and I mean, man, I started talking a blue streak like there was blue smoke on the floor, and the Empress just lies back and said, "Gimme some, man," and I thought,

Oh Jesus, where are you when what counts is dead. There she was wanting me and I was trying to get hold of myself for all I was worth, which wasn't much since I was so soft, stalling with little whispers and *oodlie-koos, oodlie-koos.* And then I heard a bell ringing. "What in hell is that?" I yelled.

"Crown Life."

"What?"

"The insurance company next door, they got recorded bells that play over a loudspeaker every hour on the hour."

"My God," I sighed, playing for time, and so I sang out, "The bells are ringing for me and my gal." She opened her legs again and pulled me down and then she hooked her ankles over the small of my back and for a moment my mind went blank. I mean blank. No zip on the radar screen. And I had this strange feeling I was on a child's rocking horse. She was whispering little love words, rocking me in her arms, kissing my neck, and I was on a wooden horse going nowhere. And those blades of light came through the slat blinds, cutting my eyes, cutting into me, and I felt a little thickening. A little rise, and she was reaching for me and I eased into her and told myself that I had to keep moving, that I had to think about something else, either nothing or the whole world, hoping I'd harden up, and I opened my eyes and saw in the light of the slat blinds that the headboard was a bookshelf packed with paperbacks. I got this terrific rush of relief. "Oh, God I want you," she sighed, and I thought if I could keep moving and remove my mind from my body, then maybe my body wouldn't let me down. It'd just keep going like I was not there and she was. So I began reading the names of the books, all my concentration on the book titles as I read back and forth across the shelf, worried in my mind, my hips humping up and down and I heard her little moan, but there was nothing there, not a title I knew, not a book, and I slumped and stalled and came to a dead halt because what little I had was leaving me.

I had nothing to say. There were tears in her eyes but she brushed them away. I stood up, feeling small. She lay staring at me. I shrugged like Sheepish was my middle name, like there was no way out of the silence. "So, say something," she said, hunched forward, pinching the sheets, leaving puckers and creases.

"Come on," she said. "I been figuring all this time on us being together and I make the play and now you got nothing to say?"

"What's to say"

"You could say you're sorry."

"Okay. I'm sorry," I said, standing still, my eyes closed.

"I hate men who say they're sorry," she cried, standing up and stepping into her sling-back shoes with those fine looking legs. I stood there with my hands on my hips staring at the loose, rumpled sheet, each crease a little ripple, as if I was out beside my window looking down on the lake.

"Anything but sorry," she said, screwing up her mouth. "You could of said anything but sorry. That's the pits."

She suddenly leapt around the bed and hustled all my clothes and shoes into her arms.

"Come on, Angel," I said and held out my hand, letting her see how helpless I felt, like I'd lucked out and lost my touch. But she opened the door, so I tried laughing but she didn't laugh back.

"I told you not to hurt me," she said. "I believed in you, so you get out of here." And she threw my clothes and shoes into the hall.

"Okay, I'm not sorry," I said.

"Then what are you?" she cried.

"How the fuck should I know," I shouted like I was angry but I didn't know what else to say.

"You just sank like a stone," she said, stepping aside so I could pass. And even though I was bald-ass naked, I took one step, and another, and then I was out in the hall, staring in at her. She slammed the door, slammed the door on my bare butt. I could feel a real head cold coming on. "I ain't going to catch my death for you," I yelled. So I circled around real quick, picking up my clothes. My socks were back beside the bed, I could see them clear as day, and I was going to have to go barefoot in my shoes. I hustled up, afraid someone would call the cops and report there was a man exposing himself in the hall, and to save time, POW, I pulled on my trousers real quick and put my jockey shorts in my pocket. But there was nothing I could do about my bare feet. Luckily, my tie was knotted and I slipped it over my head, tightening it at my throat, like no problem, man, and strode down the hall, and if I'd only had my socks on I would have been cool as the breeze which ain't half-bad at all, touch stone.

Silent Music

HE WOKE IN THE MORNING AND HAD A LITTLE ORANGE juice. Then he went out to the enclosed front porch of the old family house, a yellow frame house with a peaked slate roof. He sat in his ladderback chair and stared at the rag rug and then he went up to the window and stood close to the glass, looking into the pane, listening *to the birdsong along the back of my earbone, the soundless sound mother said was heaven sent, sitting in her hair curlers in front of the window with the old lace curtains frittered to pieces from too much sunlight and washing, staring through strings of light and pinholes at the black dog out there on the other side of the window, and unless your eye hears the dog's lower lip dripping spittle, his tongue hanging there between two white teeth, unless you hear his breathing how can you know the heat of him on your hand like the heat from the firebox when I was a boy,* Ansel Mohr in his mid-thirties, *and mother had her own birdsong along the back of her earbone, tapping it out on her little triangle in the old folks' band like an inkling of something left out of her life when she knew what was left out was love, except she always called me her love-child since a father was nowhere, never known by me, so I guess what was left out was the word of love spoken,* which he had heard on a cold winter

145

night when he was a child, the firebox in the kitchen blazing, and she was huddled over the telephone, talking in a low voice:

"I am grateful, you know that, but it's been hard, so alone, and never your voice even, let alone a touch."

Ansel had gone into his bedroom, to the bunk bed his mother had bought on sale, saying, "It'll give you an extra place to play, like a sandbox, a little bed-box in the sky," and sometimes he slept on the bottom, sometimes on top, always aware there was an empty box above or below, and he found his teddy bear under the bed. He loved his teddy bear. He slept with the bear every night. Then he went to the bathroom. He took his mother's only bottle of perfume and doused the bear. He waited until she had hung up, sitting in the shadows with her head in her hand, staring at the floor. He gave her the bear. Surprised, she held the bear at arm's length, startled by the scent, and then, seeing the empty bottle in his hand, she flew into a fury. She squeezed the bear and it cried and she opened the firebox door and hurled the bear into the fire, where, for a second, he saw it come alive as a torch, on its back, and he closed his eyes as she slammed the door and went to bed. Early in the cold morning, when the fire was out and before she woke, he opened the grate and sifted the ashes and found a small round silver voice-box filled with little holes which he wrapped in a white handkerchief because he thought it was the teddy bear's heart, *and sometimes I listened as if the pock-marked moon could speak, a peering eye blinking as baffled as me, the echo eye of me sitting there sucking on her pain like an all-day sucker, sweat-faced in front of the fire full of disdain, her disappointment, or sitting in a deck chair in the garden, splay-legged in the shade of huge sunflowers, smiling and whispering to herself and years later I put the silver voice-box in her hand while she was knitting, the needles clicking like clocks gone crazy, syncopated to the stitch dropped, and she laid down her knitting and said, What's that, turning it over and reading Acme Toy Company, patent pending, always this impending dread, sometimes looking down at my feet to see if my legs are still there, and spinning around to see if suddenly he's there, the faceless face between my hands, lips moving, staring into nowhere in the silence, between my hands, and turning around one day when she wasn't there either,* and when she died the Requiem Mass was celebrated in a stone church. It rained. The slate roof glistened through the black branches of maples. There were a dozen parish people he did not know: white-faced women in loose slack suits, a man with his trouser cuffs rolled into his socks, and the smell of Old Spice, Cepacol and incense, and there were old ladies and men from the rest home carrying white straw boaters. They held one another's hands at the ringing of the bells, the suffering Christ with his arms wide open, leaping off the cross, ecstatic, and choirboys sang as Ansel came down the aisle behind Father Cooper and the tight-lipped professional pallbearers, a dryness at the core, remembering his mother long before she had begun carrying bundles under her arms, back when she had, over a cup of tea, told him, "Life is all patchwork, and if your father had ever married me that'd be the end of the Mohrs, but you're a Mohr and that means there's meaning still in the house, though it's not much of a house, frame and all, but the fire in the kitchen is nice, I always liked an open fire," *an open wound, suppuration of silent words from somewhere, a long line of fathers foreskinning for all they were worth, unknown, unsaid, alone in ice-cold space as we're all alone in the absence of God with only His mother, the mother of God, out there in black face, alone herself, the queen of the world* and when he was a boy, he'd found that nearly all the women on the street were secret drinkers and sometimes they screamed at each other and stomped around their front lawns. Sons and fathers were dead from the war and women were left alone. Young boys circled around their mothers' skirts, sometimes finding a cork between pillows on a sofa, or Mrs. Gladdery in her rose bushes on her hands and knees, little thorn cuts on her bare arms, saying no no naughty boy, soft and firm when she sunbathed on the flat tin roof of the back of her house and she had him run his hand along the inside of her thighs into the hollow but never let him touch her like she touched him, and one day she rubbed him saying didn't he do that before going to sleep like her little Stuart did and she said he had to promise he'd never tell Stuart and then she said, "But of course you don't talk to anyone, do you," and she laughed, her robe hanging from a spike *like the old limp red inner tubes in the garage down the lane, dead snakes, because after the war mother found a snakeskin floating in the rain barrel and three dead birds and she set the skin into the stove and nailed the birds to the porch wall and the skeletons hung there all summer when I went past a fat middle-aged man down the lane who always sat on a three-legged stool in front of the garages, loose-mouthed and laughing quietly, wearing a stringy undershirt and making endless paper planes out of a pile of newspapers, floating skin and skeletons and at the end of the lane the underpass,* a damp stretch of darkness under railroad tracks and thirty or forty trains went through every day and he used to stand under the bridge, the rumbling of the freight train wheels making him tremble and shake, the weight of the sound almost painful and yet he wanted it, and when it went away he scrambled up the gravel embankment and stood watching the caboose disappear, *and maybe father was a caboose man,* and one day his mother said, "I will say this, he could play the piano like the devil," *showing me a pile of sheet music, grey walls of paper like the grey walls of Silverwood's,* a long dairy building with loading doors and ramps when milk wagons were horse-drawn and the short street was covered with spilled milk, sour and yellow-white, curdled cheese and horse piss and dung, road apples other boys had called them, with sparrows feeding on the dung, and then a man usually appeared leading a line of horses and he stared at the shaggy hair around the hoofs, their slow walk with sometimes huge erections, and the men gawked and turned away, frowning, and the horses looked as if they were laughing, their lips curled back like Mrs. Gladdery and the laughing man behind his house making paper airplanes *and up the hill, a huge stone house behind walls,* and he knew from his mother that a man named Pellatt had bankrupted himself building the house, though he wasn't sure then what bankrupted meant *and anyway it was the name Pellatt I liked because I wanted a pellet gun and maybe when my father showed up I might shoot him in the leg, not to kill, only to wound, and when we sometimes went on scouting missions through the brush along the walls,* they got to the top of the hill, to a garden of flowers in diamond patterns, and one day a lady appeared in a long dress and Stuart said, "Look at that, a princess, a real princess," and as she turned around, Stuart said, "O shit, some princess," because, with her hooded eyes, she seemed tired and worn down, and she looked to Ansel just like his mother and the women who drank too much because they were sitting by themselves waving a lace handkerchief at children, and all his life with every woman he met he smiled sadly as if he understood their loneliness and need for a little comfort, and he became good at comforting lonely women, though he was not sure he had ever been able to comfort his mother, because even as a child with his head against her breast he had heard her heart pounding and had looked up, listening to her whisper about the colour of dawn before the sun, and the same grey, except with lustre and a little pink, that she had seen in pearls when she worked for a while in a jewelry store, and glass *how she loved glass* and a blue vase she'd bought, an egg-blue that turned rose in the sunlight, and she said, "That's the way life could be if we only had the strength, and I've all the wonder in the world but no strength, and the truth is," she said before she went to the rest home, "I've loved my disappointment, kept it close like fine silk and now I'm going to lie down in it, a silken shroud is not to be sneezed at," and he walked out of the church behind the casket into pouring rain, and a high east wind blew the rain into the headlights of the few cars going along the road toward the cemetery, past Chicken Harold's and an old movie house turned into a Billiard Academy, a stone war memorial and Heritage Used Cars. She was buried beside headstones covered with wet fallen leaves, neon crosses, and a plastic Sacred Heart on a tin prop. The hard rain was slanting, Father Cooper said the prayers, and the members of the band knelt in the pouring rain, their hands on the coffin. A woman said to her friend, "She was a Christian in the Christian community."

"Oh, and outside, too," her friend said.

Father Cooper and the old men and women chanted, "Hear us, O Lord. . . . Hear us," huddled against the rain under black umbrellas suddenly blown up and inside out by the wind, up into the air like huge black tulips, *and in the cat's eye a dead bird, like once at the lake the trees lichen-lined down the north side of the trunks, lace, mildewed green, always lace in decaying grace, and the fox snake in the low hanging branch curled around a bird's nest like an old bicycle tire looped on top of itself, waiting cold in the strong sunlight, the nest, the belly trap, her nest, bare breasts, naked little girl and how she stood there sticks in my mind, high-heeled, calf muscles hard and me hard, smiling little girl, big breasts and hunching down standing in front of her sucking on her breast, the little indent in the nipple, her fingers inside my collar fingering my hair and my middle finger hooking up inside her, warm, thumb on her hair almost silky until she says I'll do you, there on the white rug in her big white room, but you see I like you, she said wriggling, and I could hear worms in the walls and mama singing rub-a-dub-dub three men in a tub and why were dirty old drinking men called rubby-dubs afloat in a washtub, thankful for her down there prayerful between my legs wondering what to do what to do, not so much who, as why, why at all am I anywhere in this whole world, actually here* in the kitchen where he sat down with one of his mother's hat boxes.

He folded his arms and listened, wondering if the voice he heard was his own.

The phone was off the hook. He heard the low hum and then the warning bleep. He didn't know why he kept the phone now that she was dead. It was of no use to him.

He hung up. There was a saucer on the table, a slice of dry toast, orange peels in a cup, a loose mound of envelopes and bills, an old wind-up alarm clock with a little bell on top, and a big moon-faced magnifying glass. He had found a newspaper picture of his mother as a young woman, the newsprint yellow and crumbling, with no date, no explanation. The clipping had been closely cropped. She stood smiling in a black dress with many pleats. He held the magnifying glass close to the paper. She looked happy. There was a crease and a stain from a raisin in the bottom of the box. There were torn pieces of blank paper, an earring, a narrow black velvet sash, a dried-up wrist corsage, and a folded piece of school-book music paper

There were no notes. He walked down the hall to the living room and stood by the long narrow windows. There was a plate-glass mirror over the mantelpiece. His hand rested on the brocaded back of his mother's old easy chair. Then he picked up one of her pressed glass bowls, the pale shades of pink turning dusky rose and violet in the light *strange for a woman who settled for so little to like so much changing light,* and he sat humming, staring at a line of small portraits on the mantelpiece, found in her hat boxes. He didn't know who they were. There were no names written on the backs, nothing, *the grace light of zero, life saved so that it might die, like mama, quiet and calm as grass, which she stood on, heels thick and round on her walking boots leaving little holes, zeros, a voice-box for worms in the grass, black, polished, a walking woman, always forgetful of everything except when she walked alone at nights she stepped on the crack, whack, came down the shoe leather, and also under ladders, and the black cat which she cradled home even though she was allergic, her narrow sense of herself fierce like the propeller blade we used to whiz up in the air when we were kids, whirling petals like when one day a kid whipped through the garden with a short-handled broom pole and mama cuffed him so hard she split his lip, excited at the blood and cried out O God, each year goes by, she said, with everyone else getting their way, the way I learned from old Mrs. Hunter with her silver spokes on her polished up gentility Ford when there were wagons, horse-drawn, Silverwood's wagon, and horseballs on the street, and her grandson, the way he used to when he wanted his own way stand and rub road apples down all over his head till Mrs. Hunter screaming gave him anything he wanted, smiling, smeared in shit, and that's the way they make their choice, smeared in shit in the sunlight* as he went out for a long walk, browsing through the stores, watching cops in their white crash helmets like punk hoods and hopheads, their wraparound face visors, shining plastic eyes deflecting all light, and Ansel carried himself with an air of deliberate well-being though he felt he might be coming apart at the seams, and as he walked he closed his eyes and named all the stores: Swepples Drugs, Danforth Radio, Adanac Cakes, and when he went into Woolworth's he saw on the wall, over Stationery Supplies and Fine Toiletries, a painting reproduced on canvas, a wobbly white church looming up out of a dark sky full of stars like big sunflowers. He liked it, the almost childish lunatic gaiety. There was only the plate-glass mirror over the mantel, his mother's mirror, because she said it made the room bigger, filled it full of light, and she had painted the walls white to help the light but he preferred the front and back porches, *like little houses, each window a small screen alive with shadows,* and he bought the painting and carried it wrapped in a big brown paper bag under his arm. The next morning it was cold and clear and the sunlight on the deep snow was bright. He took down the mirror, unscrewing the chrome clamps. He hammered a nail into the wall and hung the painting wondering why his mother would rather have had an empty mirror than a church *no matter how wobbly because life itself is wobbly, so you need some certainty because there is nothing, absolutely nothing else mama between us and the dirt we do ourselves, the damage we do in doing damage to others,* so he decided to store the mirror in the toolshed at the end of the garden. It was heavy and he carried it out in front of him like a placard. The snow was deep and unbroken. It glistened in the strong sunlight. Walking with his head down watching his step, he suddenly thought he must look ridiculous and he looked up into the mirror but all he saw was a blinding flash, an explosion of light. He stood with his arms out, holding the light, unable to close his eyes or find his face. He dropped the mirror, which sank like a blade into the snow. All he could see was light and snow and empty sky. The milkman found him like that, white-faced, drained, standing staring with his arms straight out, and the milkman led him back into the house and sat him down in his chair and said, "Don't worry, Ansel, it'll all come back, you'll see," but he sat staring, hardly eating day after day, and some neighbours came around and talked for a while and left shaking their heads. Sometimes he got up and stood close to the window, looking into the glass as if something were there. Every day the milkman said to him, "Don't worry, nothing lasts forever, you'll see," and one afternoon old Father Cooper came around. It was hot and he opened the door and Father Cooper touched him on the shoulder and slipped inside without a word, a wistful look in his eye, and then he walked toward the stairs, his hands in his pockets. He smiled at Ansel. "I knew your mother, you know, years ago." He looked up the stairs, and then he shrugged, saying, "We all like to think we've played a part." Ansel, bewildered by the familiarity, stepped back into the living room. The old man followed, saying, "In case you forgot, the name's Cooper," and he reached out and touched Ansel on the cheek. Ansel sat with his arms folded across his chest *and whisker rubs, I'd forgotten the whisker rubs when I was a boy, young Father Kurll, those big blue lonely eyes chalking up his angles of perfection on the blackboard, the points of isosceles piercing the heart of God, three persons with pointed heads, he'd said, laughing, with all the best lonely intentions in the world giving his boys whisker rubs cheek to cheek, the affection of the loneliness of priests that I'd forgotten* and old Father Cooper said, "I see you've no TV in the living room. It's a bad thing, these TVs in the living rooms. Cuts down the talk, and no talk's no good. Black-and-white TV was worse. I hate black and white."

They sat in silence. There was a strong wind and the branches near the windows swung in the wind and cast shadows across the floor.

"I'm a Nosy Parker," the old man said.

Ansel nodded, smiling.

"Is that yes or no?"

The priest, shifting in his chair, saw the painting over the mantelpiece.

"Fellah that painted that picture, I know all about that. He cut off his ear, but I guess you know that, too. Clean as a whistle. Guess he only wanted to hear half of what was going on. That's what it's like to be a priest you know. A woman gossiping is just a loose lip, but her secret she keeps in her heart. That's what you hear in confessional, you hear the secret half of what's going on, one ear to the grille, you know."

Ansel squinted and stared at the cornflower stars, his eyes filling with flowers, spinning flowers that left him lightheaded, "And well now," the old priest said, settling into his chair, "we do the best we can, it's all you can ask," the light from the windows catching his freckled forehead. He closed his eyes and sat still for a long while. The house was silent except for the wind and Ansel heard a creaking in the walls. A crack in the plaster ran like a vein down to the baseboard. There was dust along the baseboard moulding and in the corner near the foreleg of the old radiator, a thimble *mother's little cup, needle pusher, and one night leaning into the mahogany mirror on her dressing table, looking not at herself but into the past for some clear moment, some insight into the hang and shape of things and she was pouring little shots of straight gin, a charwoman's drink she'd always said, into her thimble, giggling, throwing them back and she probably used that thimble to mend the rips in my life,* and then the old priest rubbed his cheeks as if he'd just come out of a little sleep and, with his chin resting in his hand, he said, "You know, I got a theory, I was thinking about this all day today. Of course we've all got theories, but it seems to me that any man's the hero of his own little world, right, his dreams, and there's nothing a woman would rather believe in than a man's dreams about himself, but the trouble is," and the old priest loosened his collar, "the trouble is most men have little or nothing to say for themselves, they're thin in the story line, and it's why they change women, because they've got only these few small stories they've got to tell over and over, and if they're married, why a woman knows she's heard the best he's got and there's really no more to say, no more dreams, except the woman can't ever let her man see in her eyes that she knows his life is over, and this is why men take off with other women, not just to sleep with them, but to tell their one or two little stories about themselves again, seeing that wonder look come into a woman's eyes." The old priest leaned forward, elbows on his knees, his mouth set, nodding his head. He waited. Ansel blinked and licked his lips. Then the old man, closing his eyes, said, "You ever seen an owl in a tree? You ever tried talking to an owl in a tree?"

Ansel shrugged and the old man smiled and patted his hands together. "That's more like it. I can't hardly get a word out if there's no response, and I just came by because I can't stand you sitting here gawking into nothing all alone, and since I've stood talking to an owl, you got to admit that's pretty interesting, too, because there's nothing quite like the unblinking eye of a sitting owl."

Ansel nodded.

"Owls are good for keeping down the vermin."

Ansel nodded again.

"Sometimes I think God's an owl," the old man said, drawing his hand across his forehead. "An owl in the night. Except that's only after I read about Abraham and suchlike. Blood sacrifice, it's blood that binds the old books together."

Ansel opened his mouth, and then closed it.

"During the day, of course, he's not there at all, the owl I mean. God's there, that's for sure. Of course a lot of men don't believe that, maybe even yourself, maybe that's what's going on, what with your mother gone and all, but I figure not believing's a kind of impotence. A man gone impotent is a strange bird."

Ansel laughed and shook his head, smiling.

"No. No. Not that. I mean real impotence. It's in the heart," the priest said.

He stood up and shook Ansel's hand. "Don't bother," he said. "I know the way out."

Ansel opened the door. "Home, my boy," the old priest said, "whether you hang yourself or your hat, is where you are, and you are what you are."

Ansel sat in the living room. He was sweating and he stripped down to his shorts and went out onto the back porch. A white gravel walk led from the back porch to the toolshed. Outside the shed door a wooden pickaninny lawn boy stood in blue breeches and a red jacket and the eye holes had been drilled clean through the head, and though the mouth was drawn at the corners, without the eyes it was hard to tell whether the mouth was set in contempt or laughter. There were huge sunflowers that ran the length of the garden, golden yellow heads, big dark centres, the only flowers in the small oblong backyard. He sat on the porch whetstoning an old hand-sickle. He was in a white wicker chair, naked except for his white undershorts, sweating in the stifling heat. From time to time he wiped his face and shoulders with a towel and then he drank a glass of cold milk, *the other day,* as if he were talking to the old priest, and suddenly he wished the old priest were still there as he touched his thumb to the sickle blade, *I read how a fellow had his whole yard cemented and then he laid that over with outdoor carpet, glued her down, good emerald-green carpet, and once a week he went out there vacuuming his lawn clean as a pistol,* wearing a white handkerchief knotted around his forehead in a sweatband. His toenails needed clipping. He smiled, spat on the whetstone, and patted the flat of the blade on his thigh. Two sparrows landed on one of the huge sunflowers. The sparrows were pecking the dark brown centre. *They know I'm here,* looking around suddenly struck by his loneliness, *not the birds, I mean the flowers, how I feel them feeling me sitting here whetstoning, those stems there, thick as a man's forearm,* and the sun caught the blade with a flash of light and the birds flew away. He sat very still with a wry little smile, staring at the head of the blackface lawn jockey whose feet were anchored in a bucket of cement buried under the lawn, *and only last week, cutting the two flowers down right above the root, carrying them shoulder-high* remembering how he'd suddenly picked them up and started whipping them around over his head, *waving great big yellow daisies, thrashing the empty air,* and he had got the old hand-drill and reamed the eyeholes through the lawn sambo's head *and I knelt down and looked through to those little holes of light on the other side, thinking what's that, nigger heaven? and laughing not to myself or the big sun hole up there, the white hole, white holes in every black pane of glass at night, but just laughing, laughing at the street all quiet except maybe a girl, a woman hurrying home, and how come right now I hardly can think of women, the dip like a thumbprint in the low small of a woman's back, the weight always lacking in small breasts, gone, no weight, being lightheaded and haven't had a hard-on for who knows how long, nor want one in this absence, the peak roofs of the dark houses in the moonlight, gravestones gone from mama's yard, dreaming of how I have tried to love, holding on, hoping only for a little thumbprint, some stamp, veracity inside, ice worms worming their way.* He got up and went into the kitchen, where there was a clock on the wall with a black enamel cat's face, its pendulum tail hanging down, clicking back and forth. He took a carton of cold milk from the refrigerator and carried it along the dark hall by the stairs out onto the front porch. He sat down and hunched forward in his chair, covered with sweat. He poured his glass full of milk. He had a big man's body. He got up, *funny,* and walked back through the dark house to the garden porch, *I got myself in protective custody.* He held the sickle shoulder-high, aiming the blade at something in the air, and *sometimes thinking it's my head or theirs, those sun-sucking sunflowers, just sucking up all the sun.* He hooked the sickle's point into the newel post, letting it hang there like half an ice tong. He wiped his forearm across his brow. There was a heat haze over the tin roof of the toolshed. *The trouble is it's simple. No endings. If there's an ending then everything falls into place, falls because you know where you're going, which is why I figure I never know where I'm going. Anyway,* and he folded his arms across his chest, the lines around his mouth two deep shadows, *the clomp clomp down the hall of my footsteps, tunnelling, that bewildered mole's smile of mine I see in the mirror, and then I come out here into the light that glitters like particles of snow lifting off ice except it's summer, glittering sparkles of light in my eyes like sparklers on firecracker night, the way we used to write our names in the air with sparkling wands, names, light no one else sees, and I don't know how the light hit me, like lightning in the eyes, God or a great gap of nothing, who knows, I don't know if this is God's grace or the end of everything, except how calm I feel, this huge nothing or silence a satisfaction like the wasted fullness after a woman and yet the feeling that somehow there in the glass between me and the black dog, something hangs, suspended, hidden, like a truth, putting my palm flat on the pane like it was the cover of a book and inside, in the leaves of glass, peeled back, written the way a diamond writes on glass, threads of white light, there's a word, a word that'll open up between me and what's out there on the other side.* He sat for a long while and then pulled the sickle point out of the post and ran the flat of the blade along the back of his forearm. *Something about a blade sun-heated, the feel on skin, like ice water, a shock almost soothing. I've done that, up to my neck naked in ice water and there's nothing you can think, so numb, it's just soothing, you're iced, it's the end, and one of these days I'm going to ice those sunflowers, I get sometimes so I can't stand their great big heads, overgrown costume jewelry, flowers for the way things are, someone all the time sucking you dry, and I feel them actually feel the way I'm feeling* as he laid the sickle down on a small side table and smiled. He opened the screen door to the kitchen and took up the cardboard carton of milk again and *Ansel, you get yourself ready, mother's milk, the milk of human kindness,* and he shook with silent laughter and then shrugged standing out on the porch, sopping wet, unmoving, staring, his mouth drawn at the corners *no song, singing, no one, and between the dog saliva and semen, my lost face in the light, I have lost myself in the light, looking, and all there is is compassion, somewhere from someone, a word beyond anything I might say if I could about this complete nothingness which keeps my eye more alive than ever before so that even sleeping spiders in their webs sometimes look like opals in the light, but why is what I want to know, why.*

He sat for three days listening. He wondered if the voice he heard was his own. He had never heard his own voice.

He got up and got dressed.

He combed his hair.

There was a blue jay in the tree outside the window. He had never seen a blue jay before. It was almost a week since he had combed his hair. He was surprised at how well he looked. He'd lost weight, the loose jowly flesh.

He stood listening.

I have nothing to say, as later that week he walked along the river road past a small church wedged between storage yards and foundries, and he stood inside the church, *I have nothing to say,* staring at an unknown woman, *auburn-haired and high cheekbones sitting in a pew, eyes closed, humming a low mournful tune, keeping time with her foot, a light tapping on the marble floor, the sound of tap water dripping in the night, her hooded eyes,* staring at the ceiling of the old brick chapel, a plague-procession fresco, bodies twisted in pain by buboes, flagellants whipping themselves in rage, howling with the death lurch, and in front of the altar rail a carved Christ caught in midstride with big bony feet and a haggard peasant's face with a round little mouth, a short man wearing an off-the-shoulder carmine velvet cape, naked except for a gleaming gold-leaf loincloth *and you are nothing, so fishmouthed, zero,* and one night on television he had heard a man say, "You want to know how successful someone is then just count the zeros after his name," and then he and the woman went back toward his home. The wind made a light lisping noise along the edge of the river. They went down the slope of a hill behind the ironworks, an unused path, and there were broken drain tiles, wire, a rusted bolt, groundhog holes and long rough grass giving off a chill. She stepped lightly ahead and said, "I feel just like when I was a girl and put on high heels for the first time, and when a man looked at me in high heels he didn't see little-girl legs and that gave me pleasure, being a woman because there's nothing better than being a woman," *and who knows what mama would've said to that, trying to fill the narrow rooms of her life with light, a damage done, but maybe that was the light she needed, staring into the eye of her own unhappiness, sometimes strangely satisfied it seemed.* "And when I was a little girl," she said, "my father used to wash me every night and dry me with a great big towel, and then one night when he was drying me he handed me the towel and said dry yourself between your legs and though I was a little girl I somehow knew from that moment on I was a woman, I mean, then and there I made up my mind I was a woman and I felt very sad about that thing between me and my father being gone because he couldn't touch me, and that's what I was thinking up there in the chapel, that I wanted him to touch me," *pretending to pray,* and she had reached out and touched the toe of the haggard Christ and then had begun to smile and laugh in the chapel hush, and had whispered across the pews, "What's the matter, the cat got your tongue?" *and in the cat's eye always a bird, past, to be, unalterable in the mouth of mute Christ in his gold loincloth,* and the sky was overcast and grey. She had an open easy laughter, and she said, "Imagine me saying that and I always wanted to leave a man speechless so I guess you're my man," as she lay down *upstairs naked on your back, and you said, There's blood, but all births begin in the vacating blood, and next night kneeling between your legs while you shoulder-rocked the way children push themselves through water on their backs, backwards, all sourness emptied out, the worm in me shrivelled, tasting, smelling the throat, skin folds, breathing words into your mouth,* "But I guess it is the loneliness," she said. "I just went in and sat down, cool like it was, not because I never go to church or anything like that but I was just thinking about me and my girlfriends, I mean we're all married and though we're all happy we're not happy, you know what I mean, so we spend a lot of time together, which is good, and our husbands like it a lot because it keeps us out of harm's way from men, and what for us was just getting together for a few laughs turned into more than a few drinks, with at first a little touching and then a lot and nobody takes it too seriously except it's serious and now we actually strip down sometimes pretending it's a kind of fashion show and it is beautiful you know the way a woman can be so tender to another woman, you get a funny kind of mirror sense of yourself, you know, and even a couple of our husbands know what's going on, including my own, but he prefers it that way because it's no threat to him so it leaves me sad the way we all have to do these things in life without thinking," *and what is that? to be free of thinking and empty in the head instead of this impotence of the heart while suddenly so alive in the cock,* "so I just took off a couple of days ago, walking you know. Everybody takes off." She stayed with him for two days, saying, "He'd never look for me out this way because I don't know anybody and nobody knows me and you're really nice treating me around here just like I was a princess or something," sitting on the back porch, a grey squirrel running through the hacked-up flower beds. The grass was brown. He smiled. There were anthills in the lawn, pustules of sand. She was lying in the shade on a sun cot. She had taken her clothes off but still wore high heels. She had two small scars close to her light reddish hair.

"You know what's nice with you?" she said. He looked at her. Her eyes were closed. "There's no questions asked. That's what's nice, not that I figure there's ever a real answer to a question, but I can see you got lots of books and stuff around so you must be up to something inside your head, but mute the way you are you're not always heaping it on me, see?"

She sat up. She had dark nipples and her heavy breasts sloped sideways *and what's it like with mother's milk suspended in different directions and a vacancy between the legs?* as she said, "Except there's a thing I'd really like to know, without prying or nothing, but I figure you cut down all those dead sunflowers lying out there or else you got a nutty neighbour, so why would you do that, leaving them there like dead rope or bodies lying around, you know what I mean?" He touched her breast and she took his hand and wet his finger in her mouth so that his touch on her nipple was wet and she undid his trousers, drawing him out as he lay back remembering his boy's bunk bed, his box below, the haunting presence of an absence above, and he stared at the row of empty narrow planting boxes on the porch rail, and then she swallowed his seed as he lay beside her shaping silently words she could not see, *grace light of zero,* and looking at himself, limp, *all stems fall down, and bridges,* and later when they were lying in bed, when she thought he had gone to sleep, she got up and went down to the telephone and he sat on the top stair listening.

"In the heart, that's where. A little something."

. . . .

"I know I'm crying."

. . . .

"Yes."

. . . .

She came upstairs. He was in bed in the dark. He could see her in the doorway, hands on her hips. She sighed. He did not move. She folded her arms. Then he sat up and she sat beside him. He touched her hair and kissed her cheek. He kissed her on the neck and then shrugged and let her go and she said, "Well I've got to go, it's how it is, home is where the heart is."

In the ochre lamplight, she leaned over him, her hair falling around her face, and kissed him and said, "You're in my heart, I can hear you in there." Then she was gone and he stood at the window staring into the dark caves of leaves in the maple trees.

In the morning, the cat-tail pendulum on the kitchen clock clicked back and forth. There were ants in the kitchen. There had been no rain and the garden earth was grainy. A little boy had come to the door selling small Red Cross flags on behalf of Crippled Civilians and he had bought two and stuck them through the eyeholes of the lawn-sambo. A country singer on the radio was singing *just another scene from a broken dream,* "And that's bullshit," he thought. "Nothing's broken, just bent. Altered, by owl light." It was ten to nine. He was listening. He had nothing to say and stood up, looking out the window. He preferred glass in the dusktime, the ebony reflection he could see of himself and also see through as if he held all the landscape inside himself, the way he held his mother's words before she went into the rest home, "And you are groping," she had said, "and groping's no good. It pours down on you, I can see the dark right there in your eyes, which is wrong because the sky's got a glaze, and if you look up you can see that. Look up. Anybody can see that, while I got what's important to me right here in these bundles, and I need a rest and when you need a rest you go to where people rest, which is a rest home, so that's where I'm going."

She had moved into the home, burning old dresses and all her high-heel shoes in the firebox, and she had also burned a carton of papers, a quilted blanket, and a small lace tablecloth smelling of mothballs *sitting spread-legged on her three-legged stool, and where was the fat-bellied man in the stringy undershirt making paper airplanes sitting on his stool surrounded by rubber snakes and mama laughing at the snake in the tree and the gulls down by the lake,* and the rest home was down by the lake, so she always saw seagulls with slate-grey wings ripping at dead fish, dead from eels and oil slick. There was an old empty wooden shack on the beach and each morning she went down the path between tall pine trees, carrying her bundles. She kept her stool in the shack and sat and waited until the sun burned away the mist. The gulls came with the glare. She cradled her bundles against her breast and sometimes scullers appeared on the water from the rowing club, men hunched forward and skimming the water, their blades nicking the water, "And you don't know why I'm thinking what I'm thinking," she said, "but then it's not necessary to know. We all pretend to know too much. The more we talk the more we think we know. You're you, that's all. You are, and that's everything because nothing is nowhere and you're here. That's a fact. Look at it this way. You got more secrets from me than I'll ever have from you." He visited her every Sunday. The caretaker stood at the door. There were old people in all the rooms, *whispering like shedding light* as he found her sitting in an easy chair. "I was just sitting here," she said, "staring through that open door and it struck me that maybe an open door's like a coffin upright, you know, and someone was telling me the other night that at the old Irish wakes they used to stand the body upright in the open box right there in the dining room so a body wouldn't miss the dancing," and they got up and went into the halls with all the old people who were walking with their arms linked or holding hands, and some bedroom doors were open and women sat in their chairs facing the hall. One afternoon, he saw an old man with pure white hair embracing an old woman. She was wearing a pale blue dress. The old woman was fumbling with his trousers.

"Some things never die," his mother said, shifting the bundles under her arms, and she led him to the music room, glass roofed and full of light, and a dozen men and women were milling around music stands, and they all wore white straw boaters. He stood in the doorway as his mother took a chair close to the back windows, stacking her bundles, and she smiled at him as she squared her boater on her head and opened up a black leather case and took out a gleaming triangle which, as everyone else sat down, she held up, framing her face, and tapped with a little silver rod, giving a precise ping *like a bullet note, and was Father Kurll somewhere with his ear to the wall, listening, chalking angles on a blackboard, isosceles perfection piercing the heart of God,* and he saw that the saxophones, clarinets, flutes, and the small slide trombone and trumpets were golden-spangled plastic, and the caretaker, hushing the shuffling players, lifted his arm, and then they began to play *Darktown Strutters Ball,* the sound nasal and whining and yet sometimes whistling and sweet, and the old men and women hunched forward, earnest and intent, puffing their cheeks, wagging their elbows, and his mother beamed when she hit one clear note on the triangle, and then she picked up her bundles and together they walked out onto the lawn and stood under a linden tree, and there were several old couples promenading, nestling against each other, the light through the leaves dappling the lawn *and mama, she never seemed to have friends but only a genuflection before her special sense of her own self,* but she said, "You should come to Sunday Mass some morning because we play at Mass and I ring the bell when the priest lifts the cup, and I don't care much about the Mass but sometimes I think the sound is as close to the sound of God as we'll ever get." They walked through the tall pines toward the lake and the small dunes where wild plum trees and dried roots hung in mounds of sand cut away by wind and rain. They sat on a ridge of salt grass, her bundles beside her, *containing maybe a man's name who played the piano in a red caboose like the devil,* as she touched his hand, *and it was the unabashed touch of tenderness,* he thought, wondering why that morning he had suddenly stood up, taking a hammer, and striding out to the shed he had opened the door, hammering the old plate-glass mirror to pieces, the shards of glass catching the light on the ground like glittering knives, *an explosion of light in the loins of shrivelled men and women staring into the white abyss hole, fingering life, and does mama even now do what she hasn't done for years and does she hide her bundles, her secret, under the bed, breathing what words into the gumming mouth of which old man, and to what music* and the next Sunday, he found the caretaker at the door. "She wasn't at Mass, and nobody noticed until the priest raised the cup and there was no sound, and she's not in her room either or down at the shack," and Ansel ran along the beach, past the rowing club, and then he saw the seagulls circling slowly *and the birdsong along the back of my earbone, her hump of clothes there on the sand, hip ajar, one shoe straight up, pointing, the heel bottom a pinpoint I heard like a little hole letting air out of the sky, and you are, that's all, she had said, and nothing is nowhere but you're here,* where he found her sprawled flat on her back and face up to the sun, arms spread wide and the bundles free, and he closed her eyes and reached for the bundles, down on his knees, moving around them like a prowler, putting out a tentative hand, and then he ripped them open, bewildered as he dipped his hands into a confetti of tiny pieces of scissored paper and on each little piece there were notes, quarter-notes and half-notes, clefs *and all the soundless sound she said was heaven sent,* and he filled his hands, hurling the scissored music into the light, the sun high like a flower of mirrors where it glittered white, and the paper notes swirled around his head *and maybe she was right* as little clouds of notes curled and fell, covering his hair, his shoulders, and all her body, and as he knelt, inside his skull he heard the word of love. He didn't know if it was his voice. He had never heard his voice.